THE LUCKY CHILD

THE LUCKY CHILD

MARIANNE APOSTOLIDES

Mansfield Press

Library and Archives Canada Cataloguing in Publication

Apostolides, Marianne
        The lucky child / Marianne Apostolides. -- 1st ed.

ISBN 978-1-894469-47-0

        1. Greece--History--Occupation, 1941-1944--Fiction.
2. Greece--History--Civil War, 1944-1949--Fiction. I. Title.

PS8601.P58L83 2010   C813'.6   C2010-901313-1

Editor: Stuart Ross
Design: Denis De Klerck
Author Photograph: Jorjas Photography
www.jorjasphotography.com

The lines from Homer's *The Odyssey* are quoted from Robert Fitzgerald's translation
(Doubleday, 1961). The lines from the Holy Week liturgy are quoted from Leonidas
Contos's translation, in *The Services for Holy Week and Easter* (Narthex Press, 1999).
The author gratefully acknowledges the support of the Canada Council for the Arts and
the Toronto Arts Council.

The publication of *The Lucky Child* has been generously supported by
the Canada Council for the Arts and the Ontario Arts Council.

ONTARIO ARTS COUNCIL Canada Council Conseil des Arts
CONSEIL DES ARTS DE L'ONTARIO for the Arts du Canada

Mansfield Press Inc.
25 Mansfield Avenue, Toronto, Ontario, Canada M6J 2A9
Publisher: Denis De Klerck
www.mansfieldpress.net

Contents

For my father,
James Apostolides

Prologue: Five Minutes

Thessaloniki, Greece

June 1932

The pulse was unmistakable.

The doctor slid the disc across Mary's skin; he listened again. Mary heard nothing till he snapped off the stethoscope.

"Just wait here a moment, Mary," he said.

Dr. Costa Kavanidis stepped from the room. In the interval of the door's swing, Mary saw Agamemnon in the hallway, reading a report, his fingers pinching his lower lip. The door closed.

Mary looked up at the ceiling, her lower back aching on the exam-room cot. She listened to the men outside greet each other with casual confidence. She sighed, just to hear herself make a sound. She waited.

In the hallway, the men discussed work—the recent army purges, promotions, reshufflings. This latest round would benefit them both.

"Tell me, Costa," Agamemnon eventually asked. "Tell me about the exam."

"The exam..."

Costa had delivered Mary's first baby the previous year; two months ago, when Mary was miscarrying, he had conducted the surgery to remove the dead fetus. He hadn't realized, at the time, that the fetus was a twin.

"I knew it," Agamemnon said. "In the last few weeks, I knew...." He smiled, recalling how Mary felt beside him, in bed, beneath him. "It was obvious."

"But," Costa cautioned, "as a doctor and a friend, I need to warn you, Agamemnon: the surgery wasn't simple. This fetus might have been damaged." Costa paused. "You *do* have another option. You understand this, yes?"

"No, Costa. There is no option with this child. This is a lucky child, a strong child—he's proven that already. No...this child will be born."

With that, Agamemnon entered the exam room. He kissed his wife's forehead and lips; he made her wait as he cupped the swollen curve of her body. "My love," he said, "I have news."

Part I: Seven Days

Thessaloniki, Greece

April 3-9, 1939

One
April 3, 1939

Taki stood on the front steps of his house, his hand on the black iron railing. He was scanning the streets, searching for his uncle in the tangle of people who passed. He couldn't quite remember what his uncle looked like.

"Is Uncle Philip here yet?" Loukia asked, skipping from the house.

"Not yet."

"Not yet, Mama!" Loukia called, skipping back inside.

Taki watched a spider curl under the railing. The metal was hot, having absorbed the full day's sun. At the base of the railing, Agamemnon's horse was tied fast; further down the sidewalk, the Armenian grocer was pouring a pan of roasted coffee into a shallow bin.

"Hello, Taki!" Levon called, spreading the beans evenly along the wooden planks. "Is your uncle here yet?"

"Not yet."

"He'll be here soon, I'm sure."

"I hope so. He's supposed to go to church with us, so..." Taki's pinky finger twitched, tickled by the leg of the spider. "So..."

Taki created a game against himself: his uncle would arrive in time to go to church with them if—and *only* if—he was able to keep his hand on the hot railing. Taki placed his small finger down.

"Hello, Taki," Katarina said from the street, blowing him a kiss. Her other hand rested on the steady arm of her husband, Dr. Costa Kavadinis. "Has your famous uncle arrived yet?"

"My famous...? I don't..."

"Well, tell your mother I said hello. I'll see you at church."

She walked on, her skirt swooshing with each step of her high-heeled shoes.

"I will," Taki called, though Costa was already leading his wife across the street. A horse and cart stopped to let the couple pass. The driver picked a cherry from the basket beside him; with his front teeth, he bit the red fruit off its stem and chewed, open-mouthed. A trolley car rang its bell.

"Where is he, anyway?" Taki heard the grating voice of his grandmother from inside the house. His mother's response was muffled; his grandfather said nothing.

Taki lifted all five fingers off the railing, keeping his palm in constant contact. This might have been cheating but wasn't, he decided.

"Has he arrived yet?" called Nikos Gondicas, his school's principal, from the house next door. "The track competition is done, correct?"

"Yes, sir."

"Did he win anything?"

"I don't know yet. He did, I'm sure, or...probably he did. Or..."

Gondicas pursed his lips and stooped to pluck a discarded handkerchief off his yard. Even though he'd closed his school for Holy Week, he wore the same thick pants and white shirt, the same gold pen in his breast pocket. He wiped some sweat off his forehead as his mother walked cautiously outside, wearing her bathrobe. She snipped some flowers for her vase and patted her son's broad back.

"Shall we prepare for church?" Gondicas asked, opening the door for his mother.

By now, Taki felt a radiating slash of pain across his palm. He thought he could feel the bones, too: tiny hard bones, leading to his wrist, where they almost came together but didn't. They stayed separate, those little bones, and...

Spiros strolled by with a pretty lady. He was smoking, she was laughing; both had tilted their heads back, lips parted. A young man overtook them. He was walking toward the gate of the house—averting a boy on a bicycle, sidestepping, lightly, Levon's wooden bin. Taki rose onto tiptoe: perhaps this was—he was, perhaps—could he be...? But the man kept walking. Taki's hand was hurting now.

"Hi, Taki!" a girl said. Her hair was pulled into a ponytail. She waved at him, then greeted Agamemnon's horse, stroking its muzzle and scratching vigorously down its back. The girl's skirt hung straight off her hips; her shirt was smeared with a grass-stain patch of green and black. Taki watched her leap over a rock on the sidewalk.

"Bye, Taki!" she called over her shoulder, her ponytail bouncing.

"Bye, Dimitra!" Taki smiled and waved, lifting his hand off the railing. "I'll see you—"

"Let's go, Taki," Mary snapped. Her disappointment had turned to anger, turned on him. "It's time to get ready for church."

Taki followed his mother inside, his numb hand stuffed in the pocket of his shorts.

Two
April 4, 1939

The sun was high but not hot; shadows slunk close to the objects that anchored them. Philip unzipped a black leather pouch. He removed some tobacco and papers, then started rolling a cigarette. He didn't see Taki, who sat on a bench in the yard's corner, beneath a fig tree. Taki had waited all morning for his uncle to wake up. He waved, but the tree's glossy leaves opened downward, obscuring him.

Philip licked the long edge of his paper and sealed the cigarette. "You have a light?" he asked, nudging his chin toward the young man who stood on the top-floor balcony of the apartment building next door.

"Yup," Spiros said, bending over the railing, his cigarette between his fingers. "You need one?"

"Desperately," Philip said, feigning weakness.

Spiros took a drag and dug into his pocket. His waistband inched down to reveal a sliver of skin and short black hairs. He wasn't fit like Philip; his muscles were strong and responsive, but only because of his age. "Here you go," he said, tossing the matches haphazardly over the balcony. Philip reached, twisting his torso, catching the small box just before it hit the ground. "Thanks—I'll be sure to get them back to you."

"Keep 'em," Spiros said, squinting as he took another drag.

Philip lit his cigarette. He took the first full inhale, his body leaning back into the trunk of an apricot tree. As he exhaled, he offered his face upward, toward the noon sun.

"Hi, Uncle Philip," Taki said.

Philip's eyes popped open. "You scared me, kid!"

Taki gripped a handmade rag ball in his hands. "Sorry. I didn't mean—"

"Don't worry, kid. I was startled, that's all." Philip pushed off the tree, hips first, and approached his nephew. "So," he said. "You like soccer?"

Taki nodded.

"Want me to teach you how to dribble like a pro?"

"Could you—really?" Taki thought about the trophy he'd seen that morning, centred on the parlour table, beside an ashtray and a bottle of ouzo. That was his first evidence that his uncle had actually arrived. "Like a pro?"

Philip shrugged. "It's easy. It's all about the fake-out," he said. "You look one way, with everything—with your eyes, your head, your chest—everything. And then you go the other." Philip demonstrated, dribbling around Taki, who stood statue-still, though he was supposed to be defending.

"Okay," Taki said, after his uncle had danced around him four times. "Okay, I think I get it."

"Only *one* thing can give you away. One thing: just this." Philip slapped his gut, the sound sharp and taut. "You can't fake this. Where this is pointed, this is the way your body goes."

Realizing his cigarette had gone out, Philip took a silver lighter from his pocket. The sun gleamed off its surface as he flicked it open.

Three
April 5, 1939

Mary had draped the parlour rug over the iron railing. She was searching for a stick with the proper heft—weighty but not too thick—when she saw Laspiti approach in his cart. Another farmer, Mr. Alexiou, sat beside him; a second horse was hitched up front. "I can't believe he's here," she muttered. "During Holy Week." She swiped a stick off the ground. It was larger and longer than she needed.

"Good morning, Mrs. Apostolides!" Laspiti called, his voice bright. "Is Agamemnon here?"

Mary brought the stick back and slammed it against the rug, working the thrust from her belly. The dust glittered in the April sunlight. "He's in his office."

"Working during Holy Week, hey?"

Mary smoothed the hair that had escaped her bun. "Apparently," she said. She struck the rug again.

Laspiti and the farmer busied themselves with their animals. Mr. Alexiou unbuckled the leather straps that attached his horse to the cart. He tried to walk the steed through the gate, toward the backyard, where Agamemnon would perform the procedure. The animal resisted, leaning into its haunches, its ears pressed down.

"This one won't go through, hey, Mary!" Laspiti called. "Maybe you could come down and beat it through!"

Mary stopped swinging. Her dress was askew over her heaving chest. She blinked at the men, then tossed the stick down the stairs. It catapulted, end over end, toward their feet. The horse tossed its head.

"Have a good day, Mary," Laspiti ventured.

Mary grabbed the edge of the rug and slid it off the banister. She dragged its clean, dead weight through the doorway, down the hall, into the parlour.

Papou Efstratios was reading the newspaper on the couch. "I never realized how dirty the floor was, till you removed the rug," he said. He resumed reading as Mary carried the table back into place.

Agamemnon was at his desk, writing a report for Athens. As the chief veterinary officer for the army's Fifth Cavalry Division, he would travel to Bulgaria to purchase ten thousand pack animals. Dipping his pen in a glass inkwell, he wrote his assessment of the army's needs.

Given the new road into Epirus, the donkeys will only be needed north of Florina. A mixture of horses and donkeys will enable greater transportation capacity, especially for weapons and medical supplies, although the transportation of

"Doctor."

Agamemnon looked up, as did Taki, who was sitting cross-legged on the floor.

"Good morning, Laspiti. Is there an emergency?"

"Of sorts."

Taki was flipping through his father's medical texts. He liked to look at the black-and-white illustrations, dispassionate drawings of bodies whose skin was peeled away: muscle and bone connected by tendon, organs sliced to reveal their insides.

"Tell me," Agamemnon said.

Laspiti explained the problem of the horse. Agamemnon pulled out his pocket watch. Church services began at sundown, in six hours. "We have plenty of time to do the procedure, if we start now," he said. He went to the sink to scrub his hands. "Anything I should know? Anything about the case, or..."

"I don't think so," Laspiti said. "Alexiou just arrived here from Macedonia. His son has some crazy ideas—he was arrested last year. Part of a communist rally. But the father, he's a good man."

"And where is the son now?"

"I'm not sure," Laspiti said. "I'll find out."

Agamemnon meticulously dried his hands. He sprinkled some powder into a pan of water, agitating the liquid till it turned cobalt blue. This he placed on a metal tray beside some rags and knives. "Take this, Taki," he ordered. "And the rope, too. I'll need your help today."

Laspiti mock-scowled at the boy, imitating Agamemnon's expression. His face had been pockmarked since childhood; it seemed craggy and chaffed, dry even when he sweated. Taki scratched at his own soft cheek.

"You sure this is okay?" Laspiti asked Agamemnon. "I'm not interrupting—"

"You *are* interrupting," Agamemnon said, walking up the stairs to the backyard. "But yes, it is okay."

Mr. Alexiou was pacing beside his horse. Up until the day before, he'd hoped to breed this animal. He needed the extra money, especially now that his son wasn't helping in the fields. But the steed had made the plan impossible. In the last few months, the animal had grown unruly: it pulled the plow in whatever direction it chose, muscling forward despite Alexiou's commands. The reins couldn't control it; even the whip failed to keep it cutting straight lines in the fields. Castration was the only option.

"Hello, Mr. Alexiou," Agamemnon said, extending his hand. "I hear you have a problem."

Agamemnon spoke with the men while examining the horse. He checked the animal's eyes, put his ear to its chest, felt the inside of its mouth. The surgery itself would be quick, he said. The preparatory work: that's what required effort and skill—the work to get the horse down, prone, unable to fight the procedure. The rest was simple.

"Taki," Agamemnon said, crouching down to inspect the horse's genitals. "I need the rope."

Taki watched his father tie a knot around the horse's rear left ankle. The animal tossed its mane occasionally, but otherwise remained unconcerned. Agamemnon maintained a consistent, casual patter as he worked. "So we'll just tie a knot here," he said, "just above the ankle...secure but constricting...and...good— that one's done." He moved to the back right leg to tie another knot, then continued to the front. The animal seemed reassured by this talk until the end, when Agamemnon tied the rope together, completing the circle. That's when the horse started lifting its legs, one at a time, a twitch—front to back, back left, left and front.

"Laspiti," Agamemnon said. "Give me some help here." His voice was no longer casual.

"Got it," Laspiti said. He gripped the animal's soft ear and twisted as far as it would go, focusing the animal's attention away from its bound legs. The horse bellowed. Taki felt the sound in its chest: a rumbling inside its rib cage. The animal soon became resigned.

"Good," Agamemnon said. "Now—to the surgery."

Agamemnon delivered his instructions: Alexiou would hold the rope and pull, drawing the horse's legs together. This would cause the animal to fall. Laspiti would then lay himself over the horse's neck, hindering the animal's movement.

Agamemnon motioned for Taki to stand beside him. He took a rag from the tray, dipping it into the dark solution. He washed the area of the incision. "Ready...?"

Alexiou wrapped the rope once more around his hand; Laspiti shifted his weight from side to side, prepared to spring.

"One..."

Taki looked at the heavy, cushioned bag that hung between the animal's legs.

"...two..."

The sac swayed as the horse felt the gathering attention, attempting—one last time—to release itself from the rope.

"...three... *Now!*"

Alexiou pulled back. The horse's legs slid together, brought to a point beneath its belly. Its chest tipped, inevitable and slow.

"Pull hard!" Agamemnon shouted. The horse whinnied, a scream from the front of its mouth. Its body thudded against the ground.

Laspiti threw himself atop the animal's neck, pushing himself into the muscle.

"Taki!" Agamemnon didn't need to say it: Taki was there, the tray outstretched. Agamemnon took a knife and slit into the horse's scrotum. He lifted one testicle from the horse's sac, then dropped it on the tray.

"Almost done." Agamemnon wasn't yelling anymore; his voice was loud but calm. "One more...good." He put that testicle beside the other. Wetting a fresh rag, he spread the cobalt liquid on the flap of emptied skin.

"You can get up now, Laspiti," Agamemnon said.

Laspiti's scarred face was red from strain. He hopped up, fast, pushing away from the animal. The horse began to writhe; dust rose into the air around its head, settling on the moist tissue around its nostrils and eyes.

"Did it go okay?" Alexiou asked. He rubbed his palms, which were burned raw from the rope.

"Fine," Agamemnon said. Taki saw the blue vein bulging on the back of his father's hand, snaking up his forearm. "He won't give you trouble anymore, Mr. Alexiou."

Taki looked down at the tray, at the two white balls in the puddle of blood and the rags stained purple-blue.

"Wash up the instruments," Agamemnon ordered. "And put the testicles in a bowl. I need to dispose of them properly."

"Yes, Dad."

Taki returned to the basement. He cleaned the fluid off the knives, rinsed the pan of liquid. He could hear the men talking outside.

"...the beating, in Athens, by the government. Some sort of..."

Taki took the testicles into his hand. They were warm and filled his palm. He hadn't expected them to be so turgid, dense, with such—

"I haven't heard about any torture, Mr. Alexiou," Agamemnon said. "I certainly wouldn't stand for that. *But,*" he added quickly, "I wouldn't stand for armed rebellion, either. If they take up arms, we..."

Taki let the severed balls slide into a bowl. He soaped up his hands in the sink, imitating his father's brisk motions. The rush of water drowned the sound of the men's conversation.

Four
April 6, 1939

"Taki," Yiayia Loukia called, her bulk solid on the couch. "Want I ffee-co."

"Excuse me?" asked Taki.

"*Coffee!* I want fee-co!" She clamped her lips on her fleshy face. Her husband, who sat beside her, was reading the newspaper intently.

"Okay, Yiayia. But I need money."

"Ask don't me for ey-mon!"

Taki glanced at his grandfather, as if for support; Papou Efstratios turned the page of his paper.

"Mama?" Taki entered the kitchen where his mother was chopping vegetables. After mumbling a vague apology, he requested money for his grandmother's coffee.

"That's all she wants?" Mary asked, brusquely wiping her hands on her apron. "Just coffee? Not my sanity?"

"No, Mama," Taki said. "Just coffee."

Mary sighed and gave her son some coins and a small jar. "Not much," she called after him.

Taki stepped onto the front porch, into the smell of roasted coffee. The air gripped his skin—a rush of pleasure. He inhaled deeply, trying to imagine that he was Philip with a cigarette. Then he skipped down the stairs, through the gate, toward the source of the aroma.

"Hello?" Taki said. He stood in the narrow store's single aisle. On the floor were large burlap sacks filled with beans and grains; on the shelves were bins of spices and herbs—some culinary, some medicinal. Taki was staring at the hairy balls of nutmeg when Levon appeared from the back of the store. "Taki Apostolides!" he boomed. "I didn't hear you come in!"

Taki scratched at his wavy hair, his elbow tight to his chest. "I did, though," he said. "I did come in."

Levon smiled. "You did." He pointed to the jar that Taki held. "Does your grandmother want coffee?"

Taki nodded.

"Come to the back with me, Taki. I'm in the middle of another batch." Levon stepped around the counter, to the small kitchen at the back of the store. The roaster was set on top of the stove. Levon gave the crank a turn. "How've you been, Taki?"

"I'm fine, Levon."

"And school—what are you learning in school?" Levon adjusted his little round glasses, the lenses coated with oil from the beans. His fingers were short and thick, as was his body.

"School's off right now, for Holy Week."

"Of course!" Levon said.

Back in Armenia, coffee sales had decreased during Lent. Not so here, in Thessaloniki, and not just because of the sizable Jewish clientele. "So you've been going to church, hey? You've been learning the international myth?"

Taki paused. Levon chuckled. He didn't mean to confuse the boy. He liked this one a lot, actually. Taki was quiet, like Levon's daughter had been. Serious.

Taki watched Levon's fist rotate the crank at a slow, consistent speed. His forearm didn't taper at the wrist; it was one solid cylinder—tanned skin beneath black hair—elbow to knuckles.

"Christ is dead, right?"

"What—?"

"I mean, it's Thursday, so Christ is dead and He'll be buried tomorrow, right?"

"I—"

"It's a great story," Levon said. "Really."

Taki nodded, unsure why. He stared at the oil beading on the beans. "What church do you go to, Levon?" he asked.

Levon put his face close to the pan and inhaled. "Coffee ought to be a sin," he said. Then he looked at Taki. "I used to go to church in Armenia," he continued. "A little stone church. We used to go, as a family." His fist stopped at the circle's apex. "It *is* a great story, Taki. But I have other stories now...."

Taki detected a change in the store. He couldn't specify what or how, but—

"Damn it!" Levon exclaimed, pulling the pan off the heat. The metal clattered against the elements. A few beans clacked onto the floor. "Damn it..." Levon slumped on his stool and removed his glasses. He pinched the bridge of his nose and closed his eyes for a very long time. Taki looked at the steam rising off the pan, twining itself around the crank. He felt badly: if he hadn't been there, talking to Levon, distracting him from his work, if... Then maybe the beans wouldn't have burned. Then maybe...

Levon placed the glasses on his eyes. "Let's get a better batch of beans for your grandmother," he said. He walked down the store's aisle, toward the bins outside.

"I'm sorry," Taki said to the empty room.

Five
April 7, 1939

Taki surveyed the heads in church: young women's hair rippled around their shoulders; *yiayias* tried to camouflage their bald spots; little girls wore special barrettes. The men's hair was more uniform: they either had a lot, or else they had a rim. Their shoulders, though—they were interesting, sloping at all different angles. Some were like a smooth mountain down from the top of the neck. Taki didn't like those. Those people tended to be fat and slumpy. Taki's father was svelte, with a long torso and narrow waist, a set of shoulders round with tight-knit muscle rather than bulk. There were a few men like that in church. This was the best physique for a man, Taki thought.

"'Your arrows have bored into me,'" the priest chanted, "'and your hand weighs heavily upon me. Because of your wrath, there is no soundness in my flesh; there is no peace in my bones.'"

Taki was observing Principal Gondicas, who was most definitely not svelte. Black hairs crept out of his collar, onto the back of his neck, which gathered in a flap as he turned to talk to his tiny mother. Taki was entranced by the flap's movement—

"'My sores have become stench and festering because of my folly. A stooping and exhausted wreck, I stumbled, mourning all the day. My loins were burning with fever, for my life is a total mockery, and there is no soundness in my flesh.'"

Uncle Philip's eyes were closed, though he didn't seem to be contemplating the priest's words. Taki looked away, toward the other side of the church, where he spotted Dimitra. He didn't recognize her at first. She wore her hair down; it was frizzy, and longer than he expected. She curled it behind her ear. It popped out again.

"'Mother, it is of my own will that the earth covers me, but the gatekeepers of Hades shudder seeing me clothed in a robe stained with the blood of vengeance. For as God has vanquished the enemies on the Cross, I will rise anew and magnify you.'"

Dimitra dipped her finger into the wax that melted down her candle. The bead splattered, hardening on contact. She formed the trinity with her fingers, then rubbed the wax around; she liked the sensation, the tips of her fingers encased by another skin. Taki saw her slide her ring finger down the candle, catching another drip.

"'Glory to the Father, and to the Son and to the Holy Spirit; now and always and forever and ever. Amen. Holy Immortal, have mercy on us. Holy God, Holy Mighty, Holy Immortal, have mercy on us.'"

The congregation parted, making way for the *Epitaphio*, the replica of Christ's tomb. "I designed the pattern," Loukia whispered as the *Epitaphio* passed. She had been among the girls who'd gathered wildflowers that afternoon; before the service, they'd decorated the tomb with blooms and buds, still moist. "I made the pattern. It's beautiful, isn't it?"

The symbolic tomb was carried by four prominent congregants. Agamemnon's superior, Army Officer Maki Mavroditis, held the right front corner.

"Oh, the pattern *is* beautiful!" Loukia declared.

The congregants followed the *Epitaphio* out of the church, onto the street. From there, they marched around one city block, their candles casting shadows on city homes. Taki could see the *Epitaphio* up ahead, raised high. It was empty—the tomb—but only sort of. Christ's *spirit* was inside there. But the body, His body, was... Taki wasn't sure where His body was. Where it went after He had risen. He had definitely risen, so...so the body was just...just gone, he guessed. But it definitely wasn't in the tomb. It *definitely* wasn't...probably....

Taki adjusted his pace to stay beside his uncle. Philip had been gazing at the sky, contemplating the odd shape of the moon. It would've been a perfect disc that night, except for a slight deformity on the top right, as if it had been crushed. Philip looked down, into his nephew's shadowed face.

"Hey," he said, nudging Taki in the ribs. "Don't look so serious, kid. He comes back to life tomorrow: I can guarantee it. It says so in the book. It's guaranteed to happen, no matter what...."

Philip smiled then. For no reason, he blew out his candle.

Six

April 8, 1939

The house smelled of flesh. Not the fiery searing of lamb on a spit but an unctuous, ugly odour: lamb intestine boiled into a broth, globular in smell as well as taste.

The family was seated in the kitchen. They'd just returned from the late-night service at church.

"*Christos Anesti!*" people cheered on the walk home. *Christ is risen!*

"*Alithos Anesti!*" *Truly, He is risen!* others replied.

The words had bounced about the dark streets. Mary and Loukia dished out the lamb-intestine soup that would break the Lenten fast. Papou Efstratios led the family in prayer. Philip made the sign of the cross, thanking God that this was the last of the prayers for a while.

"So," Papou Efstratios said, "Philip. You've been here for six days, and I still don't know what you do."

"I'm studying to be a lawyer."

"A lawyer. I see. So you'll take exams this spring?"

The conversation felt more like an interrogation, except that the questioner had no power. "Actually, I took the year off to train and compete. I'll go back after the Olympics."

Mary sipped some soup from the side of her spoon.

"The Olympics." Papou Efstratios nodded. "I've read about the national team in the paper. Are you on that?"

Philip poured himself another glass of wine. "I train with the national team, yes."

"Ah..." This was the kind of legitimacy respected by Papou Efstratios. "From what I've read in the paper," he began, then launched into a discussion of the team's chances in the upcoming Olympics: its rising stars, its statistics against countries of similar size. "I haven't read about you, though."

"I try to keep a low profile."

"More bread, anyone?" Mary stood abruptly.

"Please, yes," Philip said. He squeezed Mary's hand as she passed behind him. Taki saw his uncle's surreptitious grab. He stirred his soup, the grey meat swirling in the yellow broth, the green oregano floating on top.

"I want bread," Taki said, too quiet to be heard.

The Apostolides men now turned the conversation to politics, as they did at every meal. Agamemnon mentioned the recent release of a well-known communist leader. "Ares is dangerous," he said. "I think the government made a mistake when they let him go."

"But he signed the declaration!" Papou Efstratios argued. "I've read about it, Agamemnon."

"You can't trust that." Agamemnon tilted his bowl, scraping the last of the lamb intestine onto his spoon. "He's cunning, that one. He would've said whatever he needed to get out of jail. Those words are meaningless."

"Meaningless for what they say—yes. But they're not meaningless, Agamemnon."

"How do you reach that conclusion?"

"They're not meaningless for the fact of being said. *For the fact of being said,*" Papou emphasized, enjoying the drama of his speech. "Ares has lost respect in the party. We've emasculated him." He made a slicing motion with his finger. "Cut off his balls."

"Efstratios!" Mary said, then looked to her daughter, who pretended not to hear.

"Don't you think, Philip? Don't you think this will play badly in the party?"

Philip nodded slowly and squinted, as if carefully considering the issue. "Indeed," he said. He tried to sound authoritative.

"I disagree," Agamemnon said. "Ares is wild. If he were an average leader—if he were Zahariadis—then I would say he's finished. But he's not. He's brutal. And he inspires with his brutality."

Loukia looked to her father, his torso angled forward—spine straight and shoulders broad—as he explained the world to his family. "I think he'll be seen to have escaped uninjured—to have duped the government. Don't you think that's possible, Philip?"

"Yes. You could be right." Philip wiped his lips with his napkin. "Will you excuse me, please. I need a little air." He left the kitchen without waiting for a response.

Yiayia Loukia stared after him. "That boy is lazy," she said, slapping her hand on the table. "What does he do, Mary? Throw a plate through the air? What will he do for a job? That brother of yours is *lazy*—zy-la!" She dunked some bread in her soup, then snatched it with her mouth. Through the entire manoeuvre, she managed to maintain her scowl.

"May I be excused?" Taki asked.

"Fine," Mary snapped. "But go straight to bed. You too, Loukia. It's late." She spoke as if it were *their* fault they'd stayed awake past midnight, not the fault of Christ.

The kids started down the hallway. "What's that?" Loukia asked. The double doors to the formal dining room were slightly parted, just enough to invite the kids inside. "Uncle Philip?" Loukia tiptoed forward. "Are you in here?"

Philip stood by the piano. One finger was held to his lips. "Close the doors," he whispered. Loukia giggled at the conspiracy.

The ceiling of this forbidden room was painted in an elaborate, romantic fresco: a heavenly blue sky with puffed clouds rimmed in rose, the warm light on the verge of spilling. Cherubs peered from the clouds, coy, their eyes large beneath blond curls. They pointed their arrows down.

Loukia hopped into the window well; the stone was thick, leaving enough space for her to comfortably sit.

"We're not supposed to be here," she said, smiling with the giddiness of imagined risk.

Taki looked toward the door; he thought he heard footsteps.

"Yes, well...it's a minor transgression." Philip shrugged. He walked away from the piano—far inferior to the one he grew up with—and started browsing through the records. "Now," he said, "let's go with something Viennese."

He slid the record from the sleeve and breathed its scent. His eyes closed. "It's the smell of elegance," he said, lifting the arm of the phonograph. "Of elegance and mystery." He cranked the wooden handle and swung the trumpet-like speaker toward the centre of the room. "Because you never know what might happen when you dance." He waltzed toward Loukia, who was giggling, giddy. "May I have this dance, milady?" he asked. He bowed to his niece.

"But I don't know how!" Loukia jumped off the well; her dainty hitch-kick made her skirt flounce.

"Then I'll teach you," Philip said, putting one hand on his niece's shoulder. "Now: I lead and you follow."

Loukia nodded. She stepped out.

"I said *I* lead, Loukia!" Philip laughed.

Taki climbed onto the window well. He wrapped his arms around his bent legs; resting his chin on his knee, he silently watched.

"Relax, Loukia. Relax and let me teach you.... If you do, you'll be dancing. Without even trying, you'll be dancing in my arms." Philip started to count—*one, two, three...one, two, three*—exaggerating the reversal of direction so Loukia could feel the cue. "Relax, Loukia. Relax!... That's it...close your eyes."

"I can't, Uncle Philip! I won't be able to see where I'm going!"

"You don't need to see, Loukia. *I'm* leading. Trust me. Close your eyes and relax."

Taki watched his sister clamp her eyelids shut.

"Relax, I said!" Philip laughed again and tossed his head. "It's easier if your eyes are closed. Don't think about it. Just let yourself be led." Philip was whispering now, speaking along with the music. "Just let yourself be led.... *One, two, three...one, two, three...* Ah! You're doing beautifully, Loukia!"

Even Taki had sensed the shift.

One, two, three...one, two, three...

Taki looked outside. People were still on the sidewalks, coming home from church, candles lighting their way. The trees were beginning to bloom, their branches silhouetted by moonlight. Taki saw Levon wander onto the sidewalk. He stooped to carry the wood bin inside.

"Christ is risen!"

"Truly, He is risen!"

"Christ is risen!"

Levon stood. Taki could see the bush of his hair. "Truly," Levon said. "Truly."

Philip and Loukia were spinning in their waltz now. The circles got tight, fast, bodies pulling together, accelerating the whirl. Philip's bangs flew aside. Loukia arched her back, leaning into Philip's muscled arm. She smiled up at the ceiling, the blur of blue and gold. Occasionally, the pixie eyes of a child angel would catch her innocent gaze.

Seven
April 9, 1939

The Easter celebration, held at the army base, had begun in the early afternoon. By now, the air was cooling into evening. The light had become diffuse, softening boundaries.

"What a beautiful day," a woman said to Philip. She was small. Even with her high heels, she rose only to his chest. "Do you like Thessaloniki?"

"There are many beautiful things in this city," Philip said.

"I'm Katarina," the woman said, extending her hand. "I'm a good friend of your sister's."

"Yes, yes. Mary told me about you."

Taki was lying in the grass. If he turned to his left, he could see his uncle's feet; from this angle, they seemed intertwined with those of Katarina.

"Mary told me you're an athlete?"

"Mmm..." Philip said, nodding as he sucked in smoke.

"How's the training going?"

"The training..." Philip said, considering how to answer.

Taki looked toward the sky. The conversation came in clearer now; the ground channelled the words directly into his ear.

"I'm not the best," his uncle was saying. "But I could be." Philip explained that he could follow a strenuous training regimen to overcome his weakness. Instead, he relied on what worked naturally.

"You seem very fit," Katarina said. Her voice was round in Taki's ear. "What's your weakness?"

"Core strength," Philip said, without hesitation. He put his

palm on his belly. "Strength right here. Because when you piv-
ot—" he reached his hand across his body "—the core is all that
holds you up, holds you steady. It's almost like it's a lock in the
middle of the air."

Katarina's eyes lingered over Philip's torso as he straightened. She took another sip of her wine.

"And that's where I'm weak. I'm weak right there, right in
the core."

Katarina gazed at Philip. He was staring out, toward his
brother-in-law, who was laughing with a young officer—a hand-
some man, blond, manning the lamb on the spit. "So what's your
strength, then?" she asked.

"The release," Philip said. "The timing—the swing, the
flow, the movement of it. Some people hold the discus too long,
so they don't get the full force of the muscle. And others, you
see—" he demonstrated "—they throw too soon—they end up
pulling the discus. Those guys make their arm work very, very
hard. Far harder than it needs to."

Katarina smiled. "So you don't need to work hard when
you're an athlete?" she said.

"Oh, it's torture," Philip joked, placing his hand on her
shoulder. He pulled back, taking a drag on his cigarette. "But it *is*
a beautiful thing," he said, "to spin and let it go. To watch it fly."
Philip's hand glided through the air, as the discus would do. "It's
almost like it's an extension of you. It's almost like you're the
thing that's flying."

His hand paused—hovered—before crashing onto his
thigh.

Taki turned his head. One ear was pressed into the tenta-
cles of grass; the other was pointed to the sky. Philip's voice was
shunted onto another plane. Now Taki could hear its tone and
cadence, but not the specific words it formed.

Katarina laughed, far away.

Taki closed his eyes into the cool blue shadows of grass. He could feel the flesh beneath his sternum dip and rise, and dip and rise, into the hollow and up again, level with the bone. He drew in the smell of lamb with each inhale. The three carcasses were arranged in a row over one long pit of charcoal. A wooden pole was rammed into each lamb's mouth and out its back end. At this point in the roasting, the lambs' lips were seared off, exposing the teeth that seemed to bite the poles, their tongues lolling to one side. The heat was starting to make the muscles blister on their cheeks.

Taki opened his eyes. His father was peeling a piece of meat off a lamb's side. The animal's belly lay over the fire. The white of its rib cage was visible.

"Doctor Apostolides," the young officer said, saluting. "I was hoping I'd meet you here today. I'm Yianni Tzimopoulos."

Taki saw the gestures—a salute, a handshake, mouths shooting open in laughter. The laughter—that came through. As did the sound of footsteps, muffled, echoing within the dirt to his ear. Agamemnon's superior had joined the men at the spit.

"Is the head ready?" he asked.

"Almost, Officer Mavroditis," Yianni said, saluting again.

"It's Maki. And stop saluting." Maki picked a fibrous flake off the lamb's cheek. There was no fat in this part of the animal. "This isn't work, Yianni, this is a party. If I didn't want you here," he said, "I wouldn't have told you to come." Maki crunched on the black-red slice of skin.

"Thank you, Officer. I—"

"Maki."

"Thank you, Maki, I—"

"Yianni joined us in 1936."

"Interesting year," Agamemnon said.

Maki raised his eyebrows. "That, Agamemnon, is an understatement. Yianni proved himself at the beginning."

"The tobacco strike?" Agamemnon asked.

"And the others," Maki said. "I've been waiting for him to get a bit more experience before moving him up."

Yianni rotated the lamb. He listened to these officers—men he'd respected for years. He listened as they discussed his fortitude and loyalty. He felt himself soaring out of his old life, into some new realm of power and responsibility. "Maki," he said. "I think the head is ready."

Yianni twisted the lamb's head in a full circle—once around, twice, again, twisting till he'd torn all its connectivity to the body. He spread his fingers over the head then dragged it off the neck, off the pole, onto a plate.

"For you both," Yianni said.

Philip pointed to the men. "It looks like John the Baptist over there," he said to Katarina.

"It's rather gruesome, don't you think?"

"No," Philip said. "Gruesome has nothing to do with it. Once the animal is dead, it doesn't matter what happens to the body, does it?" Philip picked up his glass of ouzo. "It's just not my taste, that's all." He looked across the green, toward Yianni, who was biting into a piece of the lamb's flank.

Katarina wondered what Philip's taste was.

Taki, still lying on the grass, was growing hungry.

Part II: Seven Weeks

Thessaloniki & Zagora, Greece

August 5–September 23, 1939

Eight
The week of August 5, 1939

Papou Efstratios was entrenched behind the newspaper. His daughter-in-law hustled around him, trying to tidy. She stooped to the floor, picking up broken husks of almonds by the couch. "Taki, put on your shoes!" she commanded.

"I did."

"Then what's *this*?" Mary held up a small leather shoe and shook it at the doorway of the kitchen.

"That's my shoe," Taki said, too afraid to think up a story.

Mary tossed the shoe into the kitchen, toward her son, harder than she'd intended. She brushed back the strands of stray hair that fell on her face. Composing herself, she turned to her in-laws. "Would you like to come with us to the pier?" she asked, her voice taut with attempted kindness. "We can give them a big welcome."

"I've never met them," Papou Efstratios reasoned. "What difference will another two hours make?"

Mary looked to Yiayia Loukia, who was bent forward, engrossed, sewing the final button on a sweater she'd knit for her grandson. "Fine. We'll be back later." Mary waited for some acknowledgement from these two old people. "We'll be back with Elpiniki and Stevie. Okay? Is that...?"

Papou Efstratios grunted, then ate another almond.

Agamemnon's brother, Apostolus, had saved enough money to send his wife and son on a vacation to Greece. He'd wanted to come, too—he hadn't seen his parents in seventeen years—but he couldn't afford the extra fare. He didn't admit to this, of course. Instead, he told his brother he couldn't leave the factory, even for a few weeks: business was booming, he wrote, and his presence was therefore required. Agamemnon decided to believe his brother.

"Let's go!" Mary said.

Mary hurried the kids onto the trolley in front of their house. Loukia put her coins into the glass chute. "Thank you very much," she said to the driver, curtsying briefly. The coins clattered down.

"My pleasure," he replied.

Mary stepped in as the trolley accelerated down the metal track. The driver blared his horn at a horse whose cart was loaded with vegetables; the animal altered course without breaking its rhythm.

"Can we go to the back, Mom?" Taki asked.

Mary responded with two limp flicks of her wrist. She was fatigued by her annoyance, built by hours of waiting for Agamemnon. He should've been home by now; *he* should've been making this journey to the pier, not her. "Just be careful back there," Mary called weakly.

Elpiniki and Stevie were due to arrive from New York, after a thirteen-day journey by ship, with a stopover in Athens. Mary had assumed Agamemnon would remain home that day. "What are you doing?" she'd asked after breakfast that morning.

"I'm putting on my jacket." He'd slid the top button through the finely woven fabric.

Mary had sighed. "You're going to the office today?"

"I need to finish a few things," he'd said. "And I want to pick up a car for the afternoon. It'll be easier that way—I'm sure they brought a lot of luggage." He'd adjusted his army cap, centring the rim. "I'll be back by noon."

Agamemnon had never met Elpiniki. He hadn't spoken to his brother since 1924, when Apostolus deserted the Greek merchant marine at a Spanish port, setting off for America. Apostolus was an American citizen now, with an American citizen for a wife; their son was U.S.-born, and would never know any other nationality. Agamemnon would pick them up in a motor car.

"I thought you'd stay home today," Mary had persisted.

"By noon, Mary," Agamemnon had said, kissing her cheek. "I'll be back by noon."

Mary sat on the trolley's bench and checked her watch: 4:08, it said. The second hand flowed over the 7, the 8, the 9. Mary sighed again.

The trolley car was wide. Wooden benches lined its sides, with room for standing in the middle. At rush hour, businessmen stood around the brown leather loops that hung from the ceiling every few feet. The floor beneath these straps was worn smooth from the weight of all those people.

"Aren't you coming?" Loukia asked her brother. Taki always hesitated before stepping outside, onto the trolley's small platform.

"Yeah, I'm just..."

The only other passenger glared at the kids. Taki recognized him as the newsagent's son. He was reading a handwritten note held close to his face.

"Here I come."

Taki's foot ventured onto the grate that formed the floor of the platform. He grabbed on to the railing; he couldn't yet trust this unusual ground to hold him.

"I wonder if New York is this beautiful," Loukia said, letting the breeze blow back the waves of her hair. She felt the sun warm on her cheeks and chest. "It *is* beautiful here." She spoke loud enough for the man inside the trolley to hear; she thought she sounded quite sophisticated. Taki peered forward, his torso folded over the railing. The cobblestone street blurred white and grey, as if churning in the trolley's wake.

Taki knew his cousin was called Stevie, even though his real name was Efstratios, just like Taki's was. Stevie was only three years older than Taki. He lived in New York—not the *city*, Taki knew, with its buildings high up in the clouds, and its people dashing below. He lived somewhere else in New York, somewhere Taki couldn't picture.

"I wonder what they look like," Loukia said.

Taki's body jerked up. "Loukia," he said. "How will we find them?"

Loukia shrugged. "They're family." She ran her hand along the railing, imagining that she was being watched.

Mary unlatched her purse and counted her money, discreetly: she wanted to be sure she could hire a horse and cart to take them home. She wondered if Elpiniki had ridden inside a cart since leaving Greece. She hoped the animal wouldn't shit as it walked along.

"Where are you, Agamemnon?" she muttered.

Agamemnon sat at his desk, writing a report for Maki. The pack animals had recently arrived from Bulgaria; Agamemnon had already attended to their physical needs, which were more extensive than they should have been. Unbeknownst to him, the government had agreed to send only half the cattle cars he'd requested for the train journey south. The animals had arrived exhausted, steeped in urine, disoriented. A few dozen were dead from suffocation, their corpses frozen upright, shaped by the living bodies that pressed into them, not allowing them to fall. Agamemnon was completing the report when Maki interrupted him.

"Come to my office when you're done," Maki said.

"Is it urgent? Because—"

"Just come to my office."

"Of course. Let me finish here." Agamemnon had been on schedule to be reasonably late. He wouldn't have been home by noon, but he would've arrived with ample time to reassure Mary and meet his family at the pier. "I'm almost done."

Agamemnon could've remained inside, walking through the long, low-lit corridors that bordered the north side of the army base. Instead, he took the outdoor route, stepping onto the green. A regiment was doing training exercises, jogging on the grass then collapsing to the ground for push-ups or sit-ups, then up again at the whim of the commander.

"Up! Move!"

The men jumped up and moved.

"They look good," Maki said, handing Agamemnon a glass of ouzo.

"They do," Agamemnon replied, following the unwritten script.

Maki added a splash of water to his ouzo; the liquid turned instantly opaque. "They don't know why they're getting worked so hard," he said.

Agamemnon didn't know either—not with the kind of detail Maki possessed. He sipped his ouzo. He would let Maki talk.

"The mountains near Albania are steep. A man needs to be strong to climb them," Maki said, swirling his drink.

"Have you been to the Albanian border lately?" Agamemnon asked. "Is that where you were last month?"

"No, I was in Athens last month. The only thing I climbed were the marble stairs of the Defence Department." Maki sucked down his drink. "But we did discuss the Albanian border. The roads are complete all the way to Florina."

"I know—I'm sending the mules there."

"And the Italians will be sending airplanes."

Agamemnon nodded.

The men outside dove to the ground.

The family stepped off the trolley into the centre of Thessaloniki's downtown. Mary led the children one block west, to the city's main commercial pier. "There's some lovely milk cake here," one waiter said, his hands clasped before his chest. "Soft and round.

Very sweet. Beautiful. Really." Taki saw the man smile at his mother. Waiters were soliciting customers all along the boulevard. Every café—and there were dozens, one after another, all serving the same drinks in different cups—had sent a waiter outside to lure people in. Business would pick up soon, now that Friday evening was approaching. By the weekend, the waiters would be darting through the narrow channels between packed tables, no solicitation necessary.

"Beautiful... Milk cake and coffee, step inside...."

These cafés abutted the broad boulevard, whose width was navigated by horses and carts without regard to lanes or right of way. Mary yanked the kids across the street, onto the boardwalk.

"Where will they be, Mama?" Loukia asked, twirling once. Her hair was getting tangled by the wind, the sea, its salt. She thought she must look wildly glamorous. She wondered if her aunt would look like a movie star, with lipstick and shiny-smooth hair.

"Where will they be...." Mary echoed, barely audible. She put her hand on her forehead and turned in a circle. "I can't believe..."

The gulf was kinetic: white peaks, painted boats, flotsam tossed about.

"I don't know where to look.... Where will they be...."

They were there, further down the boardwalk. Agamemnon had found them already: he'd driven straight from Maki's office. He'd tried calling home, but no one had answered.

"Stay close, okay? Stay close and look for them."

"Is it a big ship, Mama?" Loukia asked.

"No, Loukia!" Mary scolded. "If it were a big ship, don't you think I'd know where to go!"

"So what are we looking for?"

"Just look!"

Taki watched the sailors leap off their small boats, onto the boardwalk, their legs stretched wide over the gap. They wrapped their ropes around the squat stanchions that lined the boardwalk.

Other sailors were negotiating with well-dressed merchants; still others leapt down and in, catching their boats as they drifted into the gulf. Everywhere around, the waves' motion was cut by the concrete barrier of the pier. The water shot up, spraying onto the boardwalk.

"That's the best you have?" Taki heard a merchant say. The man was peering into a crate of oranges. He took a handkerchief from his pocket and wiped the sheen of sweat off his forehead.

The sailor picked up an orange, tearing off the rind with his teeth. He spit the peel onto the dock and bit into the exposed pulp. "Yeah. It's the best." A seagull stretched its clawed feet near the men, landing beside the head of a fish.

"What else do you have?" The merchant tucked his handkerchief away. His gold ring snagged on his pants pocket. "Do you have tobacco? I could use tobacco." The merchant tried to sound nonchalant. He didn't want the sailor to sense that business was bleeding, now that Germany wasn't buying Greek produce anymore. Tobacco—that's all the Germans would buy. Tobacco and charcoal: necessities.

"I got oranges and currants," the sailor said.

The seagull tried to guard its booty from the other birds that had landed.

"Oranges and currants...? No tobacco?"

The seagull spread its wings and squawked in protest. The birds dithered, uncertain. Then one—just one—hopped forward and pecked at the fish's skull.

"Exactly what I said." The sailor wiped his mouth with his forearm. The sugars from the fruit plastered his black hair onto his skin.

The original bird squawked again, strident and pained as the other birds plunged in. The fish head lifted off the ground as each bite was taken.

"Well, I need tobacco," the merchant said.

The sailor squinted, then opened the pouch around his neck. He removed a thin cigarette and drew the end between his lips. "So do I," he said, lighting a match.

Up ahead, a blond boy climbed onto a stanchion. "Look, Mom!" he called. "Look what I can do! *Mo*-om!" The boy was balancing on one foot. "Mom!"

"One minute!" The boy's mother was hugging Agamemnon. She wore a large purple hat with a feather in front. Her jewelry was chunky and glittery; it was glass and cheap, but Taki didn't know that. He just saw that it made a rainbow when the woman moved.

"Mama," Taki said. "Mama, I think—"

"Wait!"

Taki realized that the woman had been hugging his father, whose cheeks were flushed pink.

"It's so good to finally meet you, Agamemnon," Elpiniki was saying.

"Mom!" Stevie's voice was insistently staccato. "Mom! Mom, look! Look what *I* can do... Mom!"

Taki watched the boy teeter on top of the stanchion.

"Mama," Taki repeated. Stevie's arms paddled in the air as he tried to right himself. "Mama, I think I found—"

The boy fell onto the pier. "Ow!" he whined. "Mo-om! Mom, I got a splinter! Look, Mom!" The boy spread his palm flat and stared at it. He didn't even try to pull the splinter out.

"Mama," Taki said again, quiet. "Mama, I found them."

Nine
The week of August 12, 1939

Elpiniki had been in Greece for only one week—the first of a scheduled seven—and already she was feeling that scrabbling on the nerves, that need to go home. Nothing was wrong, in particular. Papou and Yiayia had been rude, of course, but Apostolus had warned her about that. No, Elpiniki couldn't complain about the welcome she'd received. The bed wasn't uncomfortable either—not exactly—but it held her differently from the one at home, carried her weight in unusual places. Each night she furled up, wrapping the blanket tight around her back. She would listen to Papou Efstratios mumble in his sleep. In that, he was like Apostolus: so far, in that alone.

"Let's buy some bread today," Mary said, hooking her arm through Elpiniki's. "Papou will be incensed that we didn't make it ourselves, but..."

"Papou will be incensed anyway," Elpiniki replied. "We might as well get something out of it."

The women were walking back from the waterfront, just five blocks south of the house. This spot was undeveloped, unlike the commercial pier where Elpiniki had arrived one week earlier. Here, local fishermen would drag their boats onto the pebble shore. They'd sell their day's catch directly from their wooden hulls, mainly to women and restaurateurs. Then they'd stop by a *taverna*, smelling of fish and blood, and have some drinks before returning home. Mary and Elpiniki had bought several trout for that night's dinner. One of the fish had convulsed when placed inside Mary's basket. Its gills had throttled open, seeking water one last time. Mary had watched the thick flap of silver skin sub-side; she felt satisfied that the meat would be fresh.

"We need lots of bread to go with this fish," Elpiniki said. She led Mary into the store that sold bread and dairy. The air clung humid and yeasty-sour. "Lots and lots..."

The women wended around terracotta urns of olives, toward the counter where the loaves were laid on wooden racks. Beyond was the kitchen, with urns of oil and fat burlap sacks of flour. The mouth of the brick oven was shut now, the charred metal door sealing off the oxygen. Baking was done for the day.

"Four loaves, please," Elpiniki requested.

"Four?" Mary said.

"One will be gone by the time we get home," Elpiniki winked.

As soon as they left the store, Elpiniki tore off a hunk of bread. "Hold on," she said, fumbling with the loaf. They were paused in front of the newsagent's shop. The owner's son was re-arranging the daily papers on the outdoor racks. He watched El-piniki bite the bread. He muttered something, his Adam's apple bouncing in his thin throat.

"Hitler's Army Gathering Near Border with Poland," the headline said, the words bold and clear. "Metaxas Celebrates 'Year Five' of the Great Greek Rebirth."

Dinner was miserable that night, again. Agamemnon arrived late from the army base; Papou Efstratios was belligerent about the bread; Yiayia Loukia kept pinching Stevie's cheeks.

"Mom!" Stevie hissed in English. "Mom, can you tell her to stop?"

"Stevie, sweetie..." his mother warned, her tone devoid of sternness.

Stevie pretended he couldn't speak much Greek. He would smile and shrug at his grandparents; eventually, they'd ignore him. Sometimes he honestly couldn't understand his grandmother: she spoke some kind of pidgin Greek, like the pidgin Latin he spoke with his friends at school—their secret code. *Riama asha igba oobsba*, for example.

"The customs are different here, sweetie."

"Speak in Greek!" Yiayia Loukia snapped at Elpiniki. "You come to my home and you speak a foreign language! You're not even my real daughter! Oh, Apostolus," she moaned, "why isn't Apostolus here...."

Mary rolled her eyes at Elpiniki.

Stevie rounded his back, trying to stretch the sweater Yiayia Loukia had knitted. She'd made it far too small. She'd wanted Stevie to be a *child*, not this gangly, willful near-adolescent.

"You look so much like my baby," Elpiniki said, pinching Stevie's cheeks again.

"Mo-om..."

Elpiniki patted Stevie's knee under the table, mouthing the words *Be patient*. She'd been saying that a lot: be patient with your grandmother, be patient with your grandfather, be patient with your cousin—he likes you a lot. Taki...his cousin. Taki would get eaten up and spit out in New York, poor kid. Taki was very enthusiastic, very earnest. Vulnerable—that was the word, though Stevie wouldn't have known to choose it.

"How long will we be in Greece, Mom?" Stevie asked.

Yiayia Loukia's hand whipped off Stevie's cheek and banged on the table. "Speak in Greek!" she said.

"Seven weeks, Stevie."

"Speak in Greek!"

"And how many weeks have we been here?"

"Just one."

"Speak in *Greek*!"

"Aw!" he whined.

"In Greek speak!" Yiayia Loukia said, slamming the table to punctuate each word. "In Greek speak! In Greek speak!"

"More bread?" Mary asked, picking up the basket. Yiayia Loukia's jowls wobbled as she turned to Mary. She took the largest remaining piece.

That night, Mary and Elpiniki decided to visit Mary's parents in Zagora. "Are you sure you don't mind leaving your in-laws?" Mary asked.

"I think I can make the sacrifice."

Papou Efstratios mumbled from the bedroom; Yiayia Loukia was snoring.

Ten

The week of August 19, 1939

The next five days ground past, slowed by the friction and frustration of trying to purchase train tickets south, to Volos. The schedule had been curtailed over the past four months, since the government lacked fuel for the train. Usually Greece bought gasoline from Romania, using foreign currency obtained from its trade with Germany. But with everything that was happening in the world, trade was down, fuel was scarce, and priority was given to the army.

For five days running, the ticket seller at the train wicket had told Mary to come back the next day. Perhaps he'd have tickets then, he said, yawning or stretching or slurping his coffee, his breath already stale.

Late one night at the end of the week, Mary and Elpiniki shared a bottle of red wine, lamenting their situation. "Welcome to Greece," Mary said, raising her glass in a mock toast. "I bet this doesn't happen in New York."

"No," Elpiniki said. "In New York there are trains going all the time. 'Track 24, Track 15...Jamaica, Babylon, Hempstead...' And with all those trains, do you think people could be civilized? No." Elpiniki poured herself another glass, setting the bottle down sloppily. "They *run*, Mary. And their business jackets flap behind them—running for trains like chickens with their heads cut off! I tell you, I expect to find their heads rolling on the floor!" The women cackled. Wine sloshed onto Mary's shirt.

"*Opa!*"

"Ladies," Agamemnon said. He stood at the threshold of the parlour, eyebrows raised at the spectacle.

"Pull up a chair, Memnon," Mary said. "Pour a drink...if there's any left." She giggled.

"Ladies..." Agamemnon repeated. "I *do* hope you're up for packing tonight." He pulled an envelope from his pocket. "Because there won't be time in the morning."

"Are those...?"

"Five tickets for tomorrow's train."

"Memnon!"

Elpiniki watched Mary embrace Agamemnon. The quick hug ended in a long, red-wine kiss.

"Bravo, Mary," Elpiniki whispered.

Agamemnon disengaged before Mary was finished. Apostolus never would've done such a thing, Elpiniki thought, pouring the rest of the wine into her glass. He would've dipped her back, smooched her theatrically. He would've made it a game. "I'll start packing now," Elpiniki said. She managed to send Mary a private wink on her way out the parlour door.

Mary blitzed about the house, packing more than was needed. "How did you get the tickets, Memnon?" she asked. She was stuffing some stockings into a suitcase.

Agamemnon sat on the bedroom armchair, cross-legged and relaxed, observing his wife. "A few phone calls."

"Phone calls—to whom?"

To the National Minister of Transportation, Agamemnon thought. Well, to the minister via Maki. "Manoula," Agamemnon laughed, "do you really need to bring *every* pair of stockings? You're only going for four weeks!"

Mary sighed, slowing down for the first time since Agamemnon had come home: four weeks without her husband.

"Will you join us at all?" she asked. "Halfway through, perhaps?"

"I can't say. That depends on work."

The blurry loveliness of the wine was gone, leaving a focused circle of tension on Mary's forehead. "Four weeks... I barely see you here, Memnon. And now I'll be gone for a month."

"Come," Agamemnon said. He apologized about the late hours. He had no choice, he explained. Things were happening at the base, in Athens, all around Europe. These were not trivial things, he explained. These things concerned far more than him. And the decisions being made—decisions that *he* was helping to make—would affect people throughout Greece. "Do you understand?" Agamemnon asked.

"I do," Mary replied. "I understand what is mine to know."

Agamemnon smiled at his young wife, leading her to the edge of the bed. "You won't need this pair of stockings either," he said. He reached under Mary's skirt and unclasped the garter belts. With the dispassionate precision of a surgeon, he rolled each stocking down, concentrating on the fabric itself, not the curve of Mary's thigh or calf or pointed toes. "You'll have a wonderful time," he said. He ran the stockings through his palm, extending them out, then laying them on the bed. Only now did he touch her skin.

Eleven
The week of August 26, 1939

"Hi, Mom!" Stevie streaked past on the *platia*, the cobblestone square where the village gathered each night. He was happier in Zagora than he'd been in the city. The village exoticized Greece: horses and carts were lame to him; donkeys led by bow-legged old men—*that* he could use in a story when he got home.

"Hi, my sweet," Elpiniki said.

Stevie ducked behind the wide trunk of a plane tree. It was eight feet around and hollow at its base, with a long slit for an opening. Stevie considered crawling inside but decided, instead, to stay out: this position would give him more options, more room for manoeuvre in the game of hide-and-seek.

Elpiniki smoothed her hand over her piece of paper, as if clearing a space for writing. She'd already written the date—12 August, 1939—and the words "Dear Apostolus." That's where she'd stopped a while ago, before the sun had slipped behind the tip of the mountain.

"I miss you," she wrote now, her face close to the paper. "I am in Zagora. It is very pretty. Your family is very nice. They are well. Stevie is well. I miss you." Elpiniki wrote in English. She'd never been taught to read or write in Greek, though she'd emigrated when she was eighteen. "How are you, my Apostolus?"

Mary's father, Papou Yiorgos Samsarelos, was playing backgammon with some friends. In between rolls of the dice, he noticed Elpiniki sitting alone, tapping a pen on her lips. She was not beautiful or elegant. Her face was coarse, with pinpoint pores visible on her skin. Her earlobes and nose, lips and teeth—they all lacked delicacy; they drooped or protruded or generally gave an impression of practicality. But this woman was fun. Papou had seen her frolic in the sea at the base of the mountain. Mary and the other adults would sit and knit under a plane tree while Elpiniki galloped across the pebbles toward the Aegean. She'd splash in the surf, splattering the kids with the pale blue water, unashamed of play.

"Waiter," Papou Yiorgos called. "A Dionysian gift for the American, please." He watched as Elpiniki lifted her head, confused by the carafe of wine delivered to her table. He raised his glass to her, capturing her wandering gaze. "Welcome to Zagora," he said. She smiled with a simple loveliness.

Yiayia Evantheia Samsarelos saw her husband toast Elpiniki. She and Mary were walking down the path, toward the *platia*, after an early-evening bath.

"Are you enjoying Elpiniki's company?" Yiayia Evantheia asked.

"Well, we had fun in Thessaloniki. It was like having a sister, but..."

"But?" Evantheia looked at her daughter, her eyes uncompromising.

"Well...she makes me wonder what Apostolus is like."

"Oh?"

"Because Agamemnon would never choose someone like her. Not that—" Mary added quickly, "I mean—she's very nice. But..."

"But to her, the 'theatre' is a building, not what occurs inside it, yes?"

"That's not how I would've put it!"

"But that's what you meant."

Mary half-smiled in agreement.

"Apostolus might be very different from Agamemnon," Yiayia Evantheia continued. "Just look at you and Philip.... Philip," she sighed.

That spring, she'd arranged three meetings with potential wives; Philip had failed to show up for any of them.

"Or even Taki and Loukia." Evantheia gestured toward the *platia*. Loukia and Stevie were in the middle of a crowd of kids, choosing new teams for the game. Taki was squatting in front of a plane tree, stroking a stray cat. He'd been there a long while; his legs buzzed toward a prickly numbness.

"Taki..." Mary sighed, echoing her mother.

The *platia* was becoming packed. People had rearranged the tables and chairs into clusters. Papou Yiorgos waved to his wife and daughter. He'd often remarked that the *platia*'s seating told a story of the village night.

Mary pulled a chair next to the baker's daughter, Sophia. She'd been sitting alone.

"And how is Philip?" Sophia asked.

"He's doing very well," Mary replied.

Yiayia Evantheia opted to join Yiorgos.

"Hey, Taki!" Stevie called. "Come on, Taki! We need more players!" Stevie stood alone, his arm circling big and inclusive. "Come on!"

Taki rose from his crouch. He walked forward, his feet blocky from lack of blood, as if enclosed in a brick of pain.

"You're it!" Stevie yelled, shoving Taki in the chest. Mary smiled, satisfied that her son was now participating in the game.

Twelve
The week of September 2, 1939

Taki lay awake, aware of himself in bed. His pyjama pants were bunched above his knees, his toes chilled by the breeze from the window. He coughed once, then sniffled and coughed again. "Loukia?" Taki said. He blinked and imagined he could hear his eyelids clicking shut. "Loukia, are you awake?"

Taki was stuck between his sister and Stevie. Each night for two weeks, his mother had warned him to sleep between the two. Taki knew this arrangement was important; he also knew he didn't want to consider why.

Taki sniffled again. The house seemed frozen; the only sound, purposeful and clear, was the declarative voice of a man.

"You awake, Loukia?" Taki whispered. His sister was curled away from him. She didn't respond.

Taki tended to be the first child awake each morning, which meant he had to climb over Stevie if he wanted to get up. This wasn't a problem, really: Stevie didn't sigh or shift when Taki inevitably nudged him on the way out. Stevie's face was so placid—with light-blue pencil-like lines on the eyelids and a strange fullness of the lips—that Taki sometimes wondered whether Stevie was dead. He knew those thoughts were ridiculous; if they weren't, he never would've allowed himself to be gripped by their morbid fantasy.

Taki put on his clothes and went downstairs, into the parlour. The chairs were arranged around the radio. Three were empty; Papou Yiorgos was in the fourth. He sat so far forward, he seemed not to touch the seat at all.

"Good morning."

"Shhh!" Mary scolded. She stood behind her father's chair, holding the back. Elpiniki was off in the corner of the room. Her spine seemed pressed into the seam of the wall, her shoulders and chest collapsed. Her hands needled with the fabric of her skirt.

Taki went to the kitchen without speaking another word. Yiayia Evantheia was there, kneading some dough, her torso rocking.

"Good morning, Yiayia."

"Oh!" Her head jerked up. "Taki, you scared me."

"Sorry." Taki took his spot at the kitchen table. He sucked in his stomach and held his breath, trying to slide into place without pulling back the chair.

"I'll get you breakfast in a minute," Yiayia Evantheia said. She poured some oil in a large bowl and flopped the dough around inside. She covered the top with a damp towel, then set it on the window ledge, where the sun would keep the colony of yeast warm.

"Are you going with us to the beach today?" Taki asked. He'd successfully manoeuvred into place. He could feel his rib cage expand against the bars of the chair and the table's edge.

"No, Taki." Yiayia Evantheia washed her hands of the dough, scrubbing more vigorously than usual. She cut him a slice of day-old bread and spooned a glop of honey on top. Usually she let Taki do that part.

"Yiayia..." he began, "Yiayia, can I pour—"

She whipped around to stare at him, her eyes sunken into her skull. Words came into the kitchen from the radio: *Germany... Poland...army...Hitler. Army* was the only word Taki could picture. *Army* was his father with his friends, dancing in their uniforms at Easter.

Yiayia Evantheia put the plate of bread before Taki on the table. She returned to the sink to clean some carrots. Her shoulder blade pushed back and forth, repeatedly: back and forth.

"I've got to get *out* of here!" The cry broke in from the parlour.

"Calm down, Elpiniki," Papou Yiorgos said. "Calm down." His voice grabbed hold of hers. "Elpiniki, listen to me. There's no war *here*. It's okay *here*."

"I need to talk to Apostolus," Elpiniki said. Taki heard several successive bangs. His aunt was lifting up books and lamps and Philip's trophies; she was searching for a phone, as if one were hiding beneath those solid objects. "My God, there's no phone! Oh my God!"

His aunt's voice rose higher in pitch; its tones thinned till nothing was left but the hum of her fear.

"Elpiniki..."

"My *child* is here! My God, my God—my *child* is here!"

Taki watched the honey ooze across the bread. Its movement was slow but not undetectable.

"I've got to get my child *out* of here."

"You will, Elpiniki. We'll make sure that you're safe, okay? Do you hear me? Elpiniki?"

"Get me off this mountain!"

Yiayia Evantheia was chopping the carrots now. Her knife was hitting the wood board in a tempo that seemed unsustainable. Taki listened to it, waiting for the rhythm to falter.

Thirteen
The week of September 9, 1939

Papou Yiorgos went to Volos to communicate, via telegram, with Apostolus and Agamemnon. He stayed in his brother's house for eight days. During that time, Elpiniki didn't leave the parlour, not even to sleep or eat. Taki watched the adults orbit around her terror: Mary stroked Elpiniki's back; Evantheia brought her blankets; villagers visited with wildflowers and bark for soothing herbal teas. Elpiniki and Stevie were Americans; none of the villagers wanted anything to happen to the Americans, not while they were here, on this mountain in Greece.

"Get me off this..."

For eight days, Elpiniki paced fast; mumbled, napped, paced slow; screamed, *Get me off this mountain!* Taki never heard his aunt cry: tears were not the natural response to this kind of threat—the kind they could perceive, but not feel with their senses.

"Get me off this mountain!"

"Let's go to the beach," Stevie said, chewing the dead skin around his thumbnail. "Let's get outta here. Now...okay?"

Unlike the adults, the kids didn't gravitate toward Elpiniki. Whenever they approached her range, they felt a push against them, a warning to come no closer.

"I'm going to the beach."

Each morning, the kids walked down the steep mountain path, as they had before the war, arriving at the sea. They would splash in the water and skim along the waves; they would play their games—their underwater tag or find-the-hidden-treasure—games that stayed the same because the days hadn't changed here, on the beach. There was no authoritative voice from the radio, no low-voiced discussions or moans. Here, everything was the same, except Stevie didn't stop when Taki said the game was over: he didn't listen to "Stop" anymore. Instead, Stevie poured the Greek sea into Taki's mouth—stop—and held Taki's head under the waves—stop—and felt his arms thrash—*Stop!*—and watched his hair flow silent...calm.

"I don't feel well," Taki said. "I'll just stay here today."

"You'll stay? Fine. Whatever the hell you want to do, you do." Stevie stomped off the verandah. "I'm going to the beach with Loukia," he added, once it was clear that he was walking alone.

Loukia looked at her brother. Their cousin's curse had made the air vulgar and thick. "I'll just see if he's okay," Loukia said, chasing after her cousin.

The Germans have overrun Warsaw, the radio said. *The British are entering negotiations with...*

Taki tuned in to the ceaseless words on the radio.

The American government is...

Those words became solid objects, sealing him into this true story, protecting him from his own imagination.

Prime Minister Metaxas has proclaimed Greece's neutrality. The country will...

"Mary! Mary, they're on the passenger list! Mary!" Papou Yiorgos ran onto the verandah, telegraph in his hand. Philip was waiting on the road, with the horse and cart. He wanted to ensure that the driver didn't leave.

"Mary! Where are they? I've got—"

"Stevie's at the beach," Taki said, standing up.

Papou Yiorgos pivoted to face his grandson. In a hoarse, quiet voice, he gave his simple command: "Get him."

Taki ran off the verandah, onto the path toward the beach. He was on a mission, he told himself: everything depended on him finding Stevie in time.

He leapt over a fallen log. The birds shot away from the disturbance; the foxgloves bent down, their yellow petals torn. Taki was on a mission. He didn't stumble. He felt the rip in his side. It was an injury—a bullet that grazed him—not a cramp: a cramp is not soldierly.

The Nazis have demanded...

The British are asking...

And Taki was on a mission.

"Stevie!" he called. The path opened out of the green density, onto the white pebble beach. Two figures bobbed in the water. "Stevie!" Taki said, running toward the water. "Stevie, you've got to go! You're going home! Stevie!"

The rush of sea and breath stopped.

Stevie stared at Taki.

Taki was seen, a hero in his cousin's eyes.

He almost smiled.

"I'm getting off this goddamn mountain!" Stevie said, slapping the water.

The rush of breath began again.

Taki stretched his legs in bed that night, no longer stuck between Stevie and Loukia. He lay awake, his thigh muscles twitching, arrhythmic. They hadn't yet recovered from the sprint down the mountain.

Fourteen
The week of September 16, 1939

The *platia* was restless with political talk. Theories sprang from people's brains, fully formed and ready for battle; often, they were developed the very instant they were argued with such certainty and force.

"It has nothing to do with us," Sophia's father was saying. He swiped his hands together three times, as if to tidy up the matter. "It's between the Germanic people."

"The Germanic people?" Papou Yiorgos said. "Like the Poles?"

"Well...but...if you look at the history...of the borders...and the demographic distribution of the peoples in that region—" Sophia's father circled his hand "—then you will see that..."

"Will there be a draft, do you think?" Sophia asked. "Of young men?"

"...you'll see that it's more complicated than a simple question of...of boundaries...because... the boundaries are moving back and forth, like the tides."

"And I pity the man who tries to pin the sea to the sand," Yiayia Evantheia said.

"Exactly."

"So if there's a draft," Sophia persisted, "if there's a draft, would that mean that..." She looked to Philip.

"It would mean many things," Philip said.

Elpiniki and Stevie would be arriving in New York that day, or maybe the next. Mary couldn't keep track. She wished it hadn't ended the way it had. She'd felt close to Elpiniki, especially in Thessaloniki, when she'd found an ally against the formidable

Yiayia Loukia. The women had been comrades-in-arms, intimate companions in their shared adversity. But those days when Elpiniki had languished beside the radio? Those days had become tiresome. Mary didn't feel resentful toward her sister-in-law, merely distant. Indifferent, perhaps.

"Your brother Vasilis is 'it,'" Philip said, poking Sophia in her ribs.

She blushed and shrank from his touch. "What?" she giggled.

"In the game—hide-and-seek." Philip palmed some almonds into his mouth. "Your brother is 'it.'"

Vasilis buried his head in the crook of his arm. "One...two...three..." he counted.

Philip watched Loukia pump headlong across the *platia*. She jumped over a stone wall, her skirt billowing on the way down. She lay herself flat in the dirt, her eyes wide against the darkness.

"...four...five...six..."

Taki had followed his sister at first, then turned back to the *platia*. He ran a few steps in one direction, then slowed and switched, not able to commit.

"They should draft girls," Philip said. "I'd want Loukia next to me in battle," he laughed.

"...seven...eight...nine..."

Taki ran close to the table. He stopped and gave his uncle a pleading look.

"You've made your choice, Taki," Philip said, his voice solemn.

Taki's brow creased. He darted into the plane tree.

"He's so serious!" Philip laughed. He took his father's glass of ouzo and drank it down.

"Hey—you should be half as serious," Papou Yiorgos said.

Philip breathed through his teeth and set the glass on the table. "Indeed," he said. "I should."

"...*ten!* Ready or not, here I come!"

Taki sent his concentration to his ears, imagining that he could hone his senses like an animal. He listened to the footfalls first, intent and loud; the noise changed as Vasilis's shoes scuffled around the tree's roots, kicking some pebbles. Taki pushed himself further against the tree's wall.

"He's gonna get caught," Philip whispered to Sophia. She could feel Philip's bangs brush against her cheek. Her breath quickened.

"Anybody in here?" Vasilis asked. His head bulged through the opening; his words disappeared, drunk by the living tree. "Anybody?"

Taki could feel the ants crawl up the soft-barked plane— up the path they'd made, black gleaming bodies following one line—pathologically precise, but never straight. He could feel them march across his neck.

"Anybody?" Vasilis blinked, his eyes adjusting to the lack of light. "Nobody," he concluded.

Sophia laughed as her brother ran off the *platia*. "Taki got away with it," she said.

"Hmm?" Philip was looking at the young waiter, trying to get his attention.

Taki stayed where he was for the rest of the game. Inside the wood chamber, his breathing made no sound at all.

Part III: Seven Months

Thessaloniki & Zagora, Greece
Far Rockaway, New York

October–April 1940-41

Fifteen
October 1940

Loukia spun in a circle. She and the neighbour's girl clasped hands, leaning their weight back, dizzy with their trust in each other. The world blurred; objects bled out of their forms and into bands of colour—green from trees and black from hair and white from the stripes on flags. The only object still defined was the other girl's face—laughing—and the six-pointed star on the end of her chain.

"No! No! No!" the crowd cheered.

Taki watched the two girls accelerate, gradually, then faster, their shoulders now hunched against the force of their own motion, trying to hold. They shrieked when they shot apart from each other; that sound was an extension of their laughter, which stemmed from their excitement, which couldn't be separated from their fear.

"*Opa!*" Papou Efstratios said.

Loukia had slammed into him; the neighbour had been flung into her mother. Neither girl had hit the ground: the sidewalks were too crammed with people. There wasn't the space to fall.

"*Opa*, Papou!" Loukia called back.

"Hey, Loukia," Papou Efstratios said. He bent toward his granddaughter. Taki expected him to yell.

"Get closer to the street," Papou said. "You'll see better up there. And you should see this, Loukia. This is historic. History is today. Right here."

"No!" the neighbour's mother called, her Ladino accent lost amidst the collective chanting of the crowd. "No! No! No!"

Loukia grabbed Taki's hand. "Let's go!" She ducked below elbows, beside aprons and skirts, through the smell of sweat and women's stockings and a novel smell, too: the grit of trucks driving slowly down the street.

That day, in the dead hour of 2 a.m., the Italian dictator Benito Mussolini sent his ambassador to the private residence of Prime Minister Metaxas, where he delivered his ultimatum: Greece must allow Italy to occupy the entire country immediately, otherwise Italy would invade by dawn. "Will Greece allow our troops to enter the country unopposed?" the Italian asked.

"No," the Greek prime minister had said.

"No! No! No!"

"No!" Taki chanted. He was jostled by his mother's arm as she waved a small flag.

Taki looked around. *Everyone* had flags, blue-and-white fabric flitting above hundreds of people. Hundreds—everyone. Taki wanted a flag, too.

"No! No!" Mary called.

A boy pedalled past on his bicycle. "Hello, Panayiotis!" Loukia called.

The boy circled back, popping up the front wheel of his bike. He reached into the bag he'd slung over his shoulder. "Catch, Loukia!" A burst of flags spread up, into the air.

Taki tried to follow their arc, but the sun had bleached his vision. Staring at the white-filled sky, Taki lifted his palms and waited, blindly.

"Catch!"

The trucks rolled down the street. Thousands of men ran from their homes, running toward those flatbeds. They weren't sure where the trucks were going; they ran anyway.

"No! No!"

"I got one!" Taki's hand snapped shut. "I got one!"

"No!"

The story about Metaxas and the Italian ambassador—the ultimatum and the one-word response—had been reported over the radio that morning. Taki hadn't heard it: the army's recruitment parade was already underway when he woke up, and Taki didn't want to miss the fun. He'd skipped breakfast so he could rush outside; he'd forgotten to ask where his father was.

"No! No! No!"

Taki's words were swallowed inside the voice of the crowd, but he felt bigger than normal: he felt like the crowd's voice was in his body, in his mouth, like the sound was made from his chest and throat and tongue—*No!*

"No!"

"Is that Spiros?" Loukia asked, pointing to the street. "That's Spiros!" She hopped up and down, waving her flag at the neighbour. "No! No!" she cheered.

Spiros pushed his way through the crowd, a cigarette held between his lips. He reached toward the bed of the truck, which was level with his shoulders.

"Look, Taki! It's Spiros!"

Men's hands wrapped around Spiros's forearm, pulling him willingly up. Each truck, like this one, was filling quickly. Men helped other men climb aboard. Then they pressed together, making more room, though another truck was always close behind.

"No!" Spiros called, discarding his cigarette. "No!"

"No!"

Taki was nudged aside by three women from the apartment building. One tossed a bouquet toward the truck. All of them giggled when Spiros snatched it and winked in their direction.

"No!"

Taki watched the truck grind past—the truck with Spiros and the other men, their fists upraised, punching out the word *no*.

No! No! No! No!

Taki imagined every man in all of Greece disappearing onto those trucks—every single man running from his house and leaping up high, smiling and gliding away.

"No!"

Levon came from his store, carrying a plate of figs.

"Isn't it exciting, Levon!" Taki said. He took a fig, interrupting his cheers so he could eat.

Levon looked out at the flags; he shut his eyes in an elongated blink.

"It's exciting, isn't it?" Taki persisted. "We're going to beat those dirty Italians! Aren't we, Levon!"

Levon pushed his glasses into place. "The last time I saw this many people gathered together," he said, "was in 1915."

"Was there a parade that year, too?"

Levon answered by shutting his eyes.

"No!"

Taki chewed on his fig. The fruit was already starting to dry—the insides more dense, the sweetness concentrated. It was almost too much in his mouth.

Sixteen
November 1940

Taki sat on the front steps of his house. Debris was still scattered around—forgotten handkerchiefs, discarded olive pits, fragments of flags. The parade had taken place three weeks earlier, but all the garbagemen were at the front, and the women hadn't yet scoured the sidewalks.

"Into the sea!" Gondicas said, saluting Taki as he walked past.

"The sea!" Taki called back.

That's where the Italians would go, people said: into the sea. The Greeks would chase them across the country, into Albania, to the edge of the land. Taki liked that idea. He liked to think of thousands of Italians throwing themselves off the mountains, into the roaring waves, pursued by young Greek heroes.

"Into the sea!"

Taki's legs bobbled in the cold. There was a bruise above one knee.

Taki's father once said that bruises were made from blood that had escaped its vessels, pooling where it wasn't supposed to be. Taki's father was in Epirus, near the front. He didn't miss his dad, who'd left the day of the parade, travelling with the pack animals by train. Agamemnon could've sat in the officers' car, but he wanted to ensure that the animals were settled, he said: they would be urgently needed in the upcoming months.

"Into the sea," Taki whisper-chanted. "Into the sea...into the sea..." He was huddled over his thighs to keep warm. He outlined his bruise with his fingernail. The purple centre faded into green, then yellow, then skin. Taki wondered if his blood was turning green inside his knee. His father said that blood was blue until it hit the air. Taki wanted to see it—his blood that was blue. He stared at the tiny holes in his skin where his hairs poked through. If he cut his skin, the blood would hit the air and it would turn red. But if he didn't cut his skin, he wouldn't be able to see the blue blood. So maybe there was a way to catch the blood that second it came out—even less than a second—that exact, precise, pinpoint of a... Just catch it, that moment when—

It was impossible, of course. Taki knew it was impossible. There wasn't a moment to catch. The blood was blue, and then it was red. Bang—switch. Taki probed his bruise.

Into the sea!

No!

"Taki!"

His mother's voice startled him. "Yes, Mama?"

She had thrust open the door. A plate was in her hand. "Your grandmother wants yogourt." Her lips were tight and turned down, sour.

Taki stood up, shivering from the cold marble stairs. His mother gave him the plate and some money. In her apron pocket was a letter from Agamemnon.

The whole world is shaking from the mountains around us. The heavy artillery is constant. The attack of Koritsa has started. God will crown the brave who are fighting there.

Mary understood the meaning of Agamemnon's words: *God will crown the brave...* These words meant that many Greek men were dying.

"Your grandmother keeps badgering me—'Yogourt, yogourt, I want yogourt'—as if I have nothing on my mind but yogourt!"

Taki held the plate against his belly. "I'll get the yogourt, Mama," he said. He thought she might smile at him; he thought she wouldn't be so mad anymore.

"And be fast," Mary said. "Don't stop anywhere. Nowhere. Do you understand?"

The Italians had bombed Thessaloniki three days earlier, at 3:18 p.m. It was now 3:25. Mary had been deflecting her mother-in-law's request for the past hour. It might be safe, she thought—safer—after 3:18 p.m.

"Just go straight there and come straight back."

Mary put her hand in her pocket. She jabbed the corner of the envelope under her nail, into the space where the skin attached.

I hear the planes flying overhead every morning. They're heading east. Do they come to Thessaloniki, Mary? Is the bomb shelter protecting you?

The "shelter" was nothing more than a trench in the ground. Agamemnon had told Yianni to dig it two feet deep—deep enough for a body to crouch without jutting above the earth's surface. Yianni's trench offered some protection from shrapnel, but it wasn't really a *shelter*: that word implied containment, safety.

"Be fast, okay?" Mary repeated.

Taki sensed the softening in his mother's voice. "I will, Mama!" he said, bounding down the stairs.

The boulevard was busy, as usual, with women shopping for the day's food. Among the women were old men sitting on crates, twirling their strands of worry beads. Taki heard the clacks all along the street.

"Hello," an old man said with a fraying voice. His strand snaked over the back of his hand, into his palm and out again. His thumb flicked each oxblood bead.

"Hi," Taki replied. He stepped into the middle of the street, toward the yogourt shop. His knees were cold. One was bruised.

He wasn't warned.

He stepped into the street—knees cold, bruised, he wasn't

warned—and then: the siren covered him. It entered him and made him run. The plate smashed on the street. The white ceramic separated on contact. The image of shattering was silent.

Taki ran, not knowing where. He followed a woman because she was running, too, and she was going somewhere, and she had a plan, and she had a bag that hit her hip with each stride, and he followed her. She curved into the doorway of the yogourt shop, with Taki just behind. There were limbs: not faces or torsos but legs and arms, pushing. Taki was shoved into an urn of yogourt. He felt it fall with him on top. The yogourt was too thick to spread very far. It only oozed, shards of red clay scattered inside, sinking. They didn't start to shake till the bombers were overhead.

Now.

Now they were shaking.

Taki curled into a ball on the floor. He watched the yogourt consume the clay.

Across the world in New York City, Apostolus read about the Greek victory at Koritsa. "They've done it," he said. "Listen to this: 'It will be to the glory of later Greece...'" He lowered the paper to peer at Elpiniki, who was clearing the table. "This is the *New York Times*," he said, "the *New—York—Times*." He turned down his lower lip and nodded, once, expressing his approval. "Okay... the glory that...the glory that...'the glory that she vanquished the myth of the invincible Fascist axis and gave to all free men confirmation of the value of democracy.'" He folded the paper. "That is something." Elpiniki wiped the table, then placed the day's mail in a tidy pile before her husband. Apostolus slipped the bills, unopened, behind the vertical stack of water pipes. "The Axis can be stopped—no one believed it. They believe it *now*, because of *us*."

"Because of us," Elpiniki said. She scraped the chicken bones into the garbage, then began washing the plates.

Stevie was playing his first football game that night. His

mother had urged him to join the track team instead. Track seemed classical, civilized. Not quite so American.

"You should write your brother," Elpiniki said. "At least until the phone calls go through." Elpiniki watched the bubbles pop in the sink. She'd added too much soap; the water hissed. "At least so we know they're—"

Apostolus smacked the table. "You're right, my love," he said, standing up. "I'll write them now." He strode out of the kitchen, returning almost immediately. "My beauty," he said. He sidled up to her, wrapping his arms around her bulky midriff. "My love..." He kissed her neck. "My doll... Where do we keep the stationery?"

Seventeen
December 1940

Loukia clasped her lapels at the base of her throat, tucking her face into the wool. The month had been unusually cold throughout Greece. Loukia wore her pleated skirt anyway, ironed the night before. She was on her way to the hospital. This was an exciting day: this was the day she volunteered at the army hospital, caring for the injured soldiers. Loukia felt her Girl Scout sash rub against her chin. Her ears stung, numbing. She walked faster, her skirt bouncing off the backs of her calves. She thought about the women of Epirus. She'd heard they carried guns and blankets up the mountains, to the soldiers. Loukia wished she lived there, too, so she could carry guns. She imagined the snow pelting her face, her hair pulled back by a crude scarf. The wind would push fiercely against her, her slight figure alone on the path beside the precipice. Her gaze would be set, her eyes locked on the grim task ahead of her.

Loukia felt her limbs strengthen with the idea of it. She released her lapels and let the cold hit her chest. Her skin was blotchy with pink by the time she reached the hospital. She was pleased that her fingers were so stiff.

Loukia was sent to Ward Two. She was shown a cart with bowls of soup and a pitcher of water. The nurse with the two-pointed hat told her to feed the men. "Get me if something goes wrong," the nurse said.

"Something like...?"

"Like if someone starts throwing up or convulsing."

The nurse left the ward. Loukia watched the hat disappear.

"So!" she said, putting all her strength into that one word. "Hello!"

Eight men lay in metal beds. Their sheets were tented up, into greyish mountains over their legs. This was the post-op ward, where men were sent after their amputations. Underneath those tented sheets were wire domes, there to protect the un- sealed stumps of limbs from infection. Some of the men had been hit by shrapnel. Most had been damaged by frostbite. Their dead muscle had become gangrenous, decomposing on the body. The men had smelled themselves rotting, though they couldn't feel any pain. By the time they'd reached the hospital, their flesh had turned soupy, held in place by their boots.

"I'm Loukia."

One man tried to turn toward her.

"I will feed you now."

For the next two hours, Loukia fed the men soup and water, holding the spoon and straw as necessary. When she returned the following week, she would meet eight others. The soldiers were processed quickly through the post-op ward—moved to oth- er beds, sent home to beautiful wives, shipped back to the front. These were the possibilities that Loukia allowed.

"Hello there. Would you like to eat?"

"Just water, please." The man's tongue stuck to the soft tis- sues of his mouth, peeling away from his palate as he spoke.

"No soup?" she asked.

He didn't answer.

Loukia walked to the cart by the window. A pitcher was set beside some glasses and a pile of inadequately cleaned straws. She poured the water.

Snow had begun to fall outside, large wet flakes splattering onto the ground. Loukia could feel herself drift into exhaustion. "I'm coming with nice, fresh water," she said. All enthusiasm had seeped from her voice. She tried to insert it again. "Here it is!" She merely spoke louder.

"*Agapoula!*" a man said as she walked past. "My beautiful Greek sister...I'm going to return to the front! Believe me: I'll strap a branch onto my stump if I have to! But I'll return. I'll fight those Italians. For you, *agapoula*..."

"And for Greece!" another man said.

"For our nurse and for Greece!"

"Please...I need water."

Loukia sat on a stool beside the man's bed. He stretched his neck forward, spreading his cracked lips.

"There you go...." Loukia placed her hand under his head, lifting him toward the glass. His hair was slick with sweat and oil. Her fingers slid along his skull. "Almost there...."

The man's lips encircled the straw.

Loukia could go home once this man was fed. She wanted to go home now. She was starting to feel the nausea—a nausea caused by ether, she decided, the sick-sweet smell of the anesthetic gas. That was the cause. If she just got outside, into the fresh air, then she'd—

"I can't..." the man moaned.

"Can't what?"

The man's head fell onto his pillow. His mouth was too swollen to pull the water in. "I..." He shook his head, a slight but distinct movement.

Loukia looked toward the door. Nurses were walking past, too fast and far to help her. She felt a stricture around her chest, as if she couldn't breathe. She wanted to go home, fast and far: she had fed seven of the eight men. Seven out of eight was seveneighths, was almost ninety percent, and she had fed them. Another nurse passed outside the door.

The man groaned. "I need water. Please..."

Loukia looked down. She watched the man's lips fall open, slack. His tongue was moving—rolling—inside his mouth. He was trying to suckle.

"I'll go back to the front—you'll see!" one man said. "This won't stop me!"

"I'll go back for you, *agapoula!*"

"For Greece!"

"For our nurse!"

Loukia focused on the man before her, his cracked lips and chalky skin. She dipped her finger in the cup of water. She paused to let the excess drip down. Then she placed her fingertip between the man's lips. She felt his tongue. "Drink," she whispered to the man. "Drink now."

He listened to her: he, a seventeen-year-old man, obeyed his eleven-year-old nurse.

"For Greece!" someone said.

Eighteen
January 1941

Agamemnon's letters became shorter as the war progressed. The notes from November were pages-long evocations of longing and love. They were like fragments of poetry.

I am shivering under the woollen blanket I brought from home. I'm shivering, but I'm not cold. Not on my skin. I am trembling from some deeper cold. Only you could warm me, Mary. The planes are overhead constantly.

Mary would read his notes and smile at the irony: Agamemnon never read anything except military briefs and medical books. She used to drag him to the theatre, where he'd assiduously study the programs, as if that's where the meaning of the drama could be found.

We were all huddled around the radio. Carafes were everywhere, filled with water not wine, but we drank and got drunk anyway. We were drunken soldiers, Mary. Drunken on pride. The Prime Minister announced the victory.

Now, two months later, the letters had become shorter, more businesslike. Mary cherished them nonetheless: they were evidence that Agamemnon was alive, or had been one week earlier.

13 January, 1941
Dear Mary,

Were you able to send the boots I requested? Mine are completely worn through. Please send lentils, too, if you have any to spare. The ones we get are half-eaten by bugs. We eat them anyway, of course.

Mary put the letter on the kitchen table. She'd sent the boots weeks ago, as soon as she'd received Agamemnon's initial request. She slid her feet out of her slippers and put them, flat, onto the stone floor.

The animals are doing better than the men. They are better in the snow. They don't get discouraged as easily. They don't have the ability to anticipate like we do.

I still haven't heard any news about Philip. I'll keep asking.

I'm sorry this letter is so short. My fingers are stiff—need new gloves. I love you.

Love,

Memnon

Mary smoothed her hand over the letter, pressing harder with each stroke—pressing, as if to push through his words, to him.

"Mary," Yiayia Loukia called. "It's cold in here. Want I another log on the fire. Now..."

Mary ignored her mother-in-law.

"Mary! Cold it's in—"

"Coming," she sighed. Then she turned to her daughter, who was boiling water in a *briki*. "Actually, can you deal with the fire, please."

"Mama..." Loukia arched her eyebrows, her tone imperious. "I'm making coffee for Papou and Principal Gondicas," she said. "I have to get it just right, or it will be *ruined*."

Mary opened her mouth to respond but her incredulity

couldn't fit through her throat. She said nothing.

"The timing has to be *perfect*," Loukia continued. She stirred some ersatz coffee into the *briki*. She waited for it to foam.

"Doubles, doubles...come on, doubles..." Papou Efstratios said in the next room. He and Gondicas were playing backgammon. Papou jiggled his fist and rolled the dice. "Ah! Never am I given good luck! Never in my life!"

Taki watched from across the room, having finished his afternoon snack. He wasn't entirely sure of the goals of the game, let alone its rules. He tried to learn by observing the men, but they played too fast.

"It's not a question of luck," Gondicas said, rolling the dice. He lay two fingers atop two separate pieces; with a loose wrist he slid them across the wood board, bringing them together over Papou's lone white disc.

"Damn," Papou muttered.

"Coffee is ready!" Loukia entered from the kitchen, placing tiny cups of chickpea coffee before the two men. She stood with the tray under her arm, rising onto her tiptoes, awaiting their response.

Gondicas took a sip and sighed with theatrical contentment. "You're going to be a wonderful wife to someone, Loukia," he said. "It's delicious, really."

Loukia giggled and looked to her grandfather. "Doubles, doubles... I need doubles," he said. He rolled a two and a three. "Again!" He slapped the table, spilling some of the blond coffee onto the saucer. Without looking down, he sipped from his cup. His face pinched into an expression of disgust.

"Mary, it's cold in here. Want I another log on the fire. Now!"

Mary clanged the door to the wood-burning stove. The pile of logs had gotten small.

Yiayia Loukia frowned and turned toward the stove. She

seemed confused. She was trying to connect the clanging sound with that big, inert object. "Mary, cold it's in here," she repeated, her tone unchanging. "Want I other-an—"

"Loukia," Mary said, "please come to the kitchen."

"—fire—"

"Now," she added.

"Now!" Yiayia Loukia paused, looking up at her daughter-in-law.

"Don't be so upset!" Loukia encouraged her grandfather. "You'll have better luck next game!"

Mary took her daughter's arm and led her into the kitchen. "Please write a short note to your father," she said. She gave Loukia a newly sharpened pencil. Loukia took her mother's pen instead.

> *Dear Dad,*
>
> *We are all fine. Now Papou and Principal Gondicas are playing backgammon, and I think Gondicas is winning. I just made them coffee, and Gondicas said I make coffee beautifully. Come so I can make you a cup of coffee every day.*
>
> *Love,*
> *Loukia*

Loukia reread her note, satisfied. "Your turn," she called to Taki, who was sticking his fingers inside a glass, trying to absorb some last, non-existent drop of milk. "Taki..."

Taki brought his glass to the sink. He picked up the pencil. He adjusted the paper. "Mom?" he asked. "What should I say?"

"Whatever you want to tell your father," Mary said, washing the dishes.

Taki stared at the paper's faint lines.

"What do you want to tell him? What do you want to say?"

"Mary!" Yiayia Loukia called. "Cold it's in here! Ry-ma!"

Taki looked at the blank spaces—four lines to fill. Four lines to tell his father...something. Whatever he wanted. Something he did, or thought. Something his father might like. Something that might explain, or give a sense of...or a glimpse into...

> My Dear Sweet Dad,
> I just ate two slices of bread with milk. I wanted one more, but Mom did not give it to me, because she wanted me to have my appatite for the evening.

He brushed the pencil's lead off the paper. He was pushing too hard, he realized. His teacher had warned him about that—about his tendency to hold the pencil too tight, keeping his hand too stiff. Taki noticed that he'd misspelled the word *appetite*. He reshaped the second vowel. He hoped his father wouldn't notice.

> Many kisses, and I hope you come back soon.
> Love, Taki

Mary took the paper from her son. "Very nice," she managed. She placed her fists on the table, steadying herself from a sudden dizziness. The heel of bread was wrapped in front of her. It would have to last another day, for the entire family.

"Snake eyes!" Papou Efstratios exclaimed. "Finally I get doubles, and they're goddamn snake eyes!"

Nineteen
February 1941

Mary turned to the nurse. "Are you sure this is him?"

"This is him."

Mary's mother had called her in Thessaloniki the previous day. They found Philip, she said. Come to the hospital in Volos. Immediately. She didn't elaborate.

"What happened?"

"You'll have to wait for the doctor," the nurse said. She looked out the window, toward the chestnut tree, its branches fingering forward. "I have to tend to the others."

Mary's heart was knocked off its rhythm. It beat fast, then paused, then fast again. She wanted Agamemnon beside her, to hold her; she wanted her brother.

Mary stood by the bed and stared at the blanket, the separate strands of black and white dirtied into a grey whole. She noticed some woollen hairs poking up, twisted into odd angles. There were only a few at first—one hooked up, another bent over— but her eyes refocused: they were everywhere now, these frenetic grey hairs, all crazed and curling atop the body of her brother.

One of the soldiers started singing a war song.

We search
aimless
for those who left

Another man coughed, twice. Then a third time. Then he couldn't stop.

We see
faces
of those now gone

Mary tried to look at her brother's face, but there was none—just the mask of browning bandages. Her gaze shifted down, toward his right shoulder, which was naked and uninjured. The muscle was defined beneath the skin, strong even in repose. She watched her hand float toward that spot on his body.

"Are you his wife?"

Mary wheeled around. "His sister. He isn't married."

"That's good," the doctor muttered.

"What?"

The doctor looked up from his chart. "He presented with a bullet in his ankle. The bullet entered laterally and traversed the joint and—" The doctor spoke in abstractions: septicemia, occlusions, edema. These words stabilized Mary. They were big and cold and biologically precise. They weren't about Philip—her brother—this man, mangled.

"He'll walk, with a severe limp. But he'll walk. Assuming he recovers from the other injury."

Let us be glad
for glory
surrounds the gone

"Tell me about the other injury, please."

The doctor wet his bottom lip.

"Was it a bullet as well?" Mary asked. "Or shrapnel? Can he recover from a bullet to the forehead?"

"It wasn't a bullet."

Let us not cry
from pain
We pray—

"So it was shrapnel then," Mary asserted. She sought the doctor's gaze, which he refused to give. "Please tell me," she said, her voice now low.

"He fell from a very great height."

We pray for your sweet return.
We await your
sweet return... Return.

"How," she asked. "In the mountains? How?" She stepped forward and put her body in front of the doctor's. "How did he fall." The nurse looked from across the ward.

"As I said," the doctor continued, biting his lip as he wet it again, "he fell from a very great height, onto a cement sidewalk. He landed on the anterior dorsal section of the skull."

"Onto a cement sidewalk?" Mary repeated. Her eyes squinted, once, a pulse of unwanted understanding.

The doctor rubbed his beard, then slid his jaw to one side. He decided to take Mary's gaze now. He held it until he was certain she'd follow, then he turned toward the window.

Philip awoke to the sound of his sister wailing, a throb that merged with the swollen pain that was now his face.

3 March, 1941
Dearest Memnon,

Philip was injured very badly. He was shot in the ankle at the front. But that's not the worst.

On the night of February 15, Philip...

Mary wasn't sure what to say next. She was sitting at her cousin's kitchen table in Volos. Her parents were asleep on the apartment's only bed. The mid-morning sun beat through the window.

On the night of February 15, Philip

Mary would tell everyone that Philip had been hit in the head with shrapnel. With her parents, she simply wouldn't refer to the cause of injury, ever. She would never be certain what they knew.

On the night of February 15, Philip

Philip what: on the night of February 15, Philip lowered himself off his bed, protecting his injured ankle. He tried to hop through the ward, but he kept knocking into carts and beds. Since he didn't want to alert anyone to his activity, Philip sunk to the floor. Propped on hands and bent knees, he crawled to the window. He placed his hands on the sill and raised himself, effortlessly: he was—had been—an athlete.

> *On the night of February 15, Philip fell from the hospital window onto a cement sidewalk. He sustained a severe fracture of the head, and both jaws were dislocated. His head injuries were extreme, and the doctors expected him to die hour after hour. When I arrived, I found him totally disfigured. It's a tragedy, Agamemnon—a tragedy.*

Mary heard her father groaning in his sleep.
I miss you, Memnon.

Mary remained in Volos for eight days. In the mornings, she would sit at Philip's bedside, knitting him a hat. In the afternoons, she'd attend to her parents' grief, holding them as they unravelled. She'd always suspected that Philip was their favourite child. She didn't resent them for it.

Back in Thessaloniki, Katarina was handling Mary's domestic duties. When she'd heard about Philip's injury, she'd offered to stay at the house, caring for Taki and Loukia, Papou and Yiayia. Mary had assumed, initially, that she'd be gone for a week, just until she could reassure herself that her brother was okay.

"How is Philip today?" Katarina asked Mary. The phone connection was crackling, but adequate. Katarina was relieved that the call had gone through: she hadn't spoken with Mary in four days, in part—but only in part—because the phone lines had been unreliable. Today, though, Mary was too tired to avoid the conversation.

"Mary?"

"Hmm?"

"How is Philip today?"

Mary still didn't answer. "What's new in Thessaloniki," she finally said.

Katarina took her friend's cue. She talked about Yiayia Loukia's refusal to bathe, and Papou Efstratios's demands for bread. The kids were fine, she said. There had been one bombing, but no one was hurt. And, she added, the family had received a letter from Agamemnon.

"Open it."

"Are you sure you want—"

"Just open it, Katarina." Mary's eyes were depressed in their sockets, the skin baggy with fatigue. "Just... Sorry for snapping." She heard the paper tear.

"'My darling wife,'" Katarina read. She paused. "Mary, are you sure..."

"Katarina, please...please read the letter."

"'My darling wife,'" Katarina repeated. "'I received the boots you sent. Thank you. They make the days more productive. I need each minute, as we are preparing for the battles to resume.'"

Katarina cleared her throat. Just saying those words out loud—taking them into her mouth—made the men's lives at the front more real to her.

"'The animals know it: the battle is approaching. They're agitated, harder to work with. The men are training more. We're not prepared. None of us. The planes have started again, regular.'"

Philip's face was lumpy, as if his skin were melting, boiling. He hadn't shown any recognition of Mary.

"'Mary, I need to be brief—running out of paper—so I'll say it bluntly: I want you out of Thessaloniki as soon as possible. Go to Zagora. Take my parents, too. If they won't leave the house, pay someone to stay with them.'" Katarina stopped reading. "Mary?"

"Hmm..."

"Did you hear that?"

"Yes—the men are training more, and..." Mary exhaled, her chest collapsing. "No, Katarina. I'm sorry...I didn't hear."

Katarina looked into the backyard. Taki was playing soccer with a girl from school. They were using the bomb shelter as their goal.

"Score!" the girl said. Katarina didn't hear the word; she merely saw the girl's arms shoot up as the ball arced around Taki, landing in the long hole dug in the ground.

"Agamemnon wants you and the kids out of Thessaloniki."

Mary said nothing.

"Are you there, Mary?"

Mary closed her eyes. "I'm here."

Twenty
March 1941

The entire village was on the *platia*—all except the men, who were at the front, or in the hospital, or dead. The people waved their flags.

Loukia was polite, but firm, as she cleared a space on the *platia*. "Excuse me, please. Excuse me, but the show is about to begin."

She had written the play to commemorate Greek Independence Day—March 25, 1821—when the Greeks rebelled against the Turkish occupation. She'd planned to mount the play on Greek Independence Day, or the day that Greece beat Italy, whichever came first.

As it turned out, the days nearly coincided: despite their advantage in men and money and arms, the Italians surrendered to the Greeks on March 20. The war against Italy was over: the Greeks had won.

"Are you ready?" Loukia asked the actors. Then she turned toward the villagers.

"On this day," she announced, "we are here to celebrate Greek heroism and bravery and tradition and..." She shook back her hair, trying to regain the focus of her speech. "And...just as we beat the Turks one hundred years ago, we beat the Italians now! The Greek spirit cannot be defeated! And now, I present—"

She stepped dramatically back, as if pulling aside a curtain. The moon was a spotlight, she thought, shining upon her. "I present *The Independence of the Greeks*, a play written and directed by myself, Loukia Apostolides." Loukia walked aside and nodded vigorously at the boys: a subtle signal, she thought, that the play was to begin.

"The time has verily come," Vasilis said, "to overthrow the oppressive yoke of Turkish oppression. We, the great Hellenic people, who brought culture, language, science and..." Vasilis's eyes darted over to Loukia, who projected one word in a loud whisper.

"Democracy..."

"...and democracy to the world..." Vasilis looked back to the crowd. His mother waved. "We have been enslaved by the brutish Turks for four hundred years. Look at them." He swept his hand toward a table of Turks, who were lolling about on chairs, water-filled bottles of ouzo arranged chaotically before them. "They rape our land and our women." With one arm still outstretched, he swept the other toward the girls, who huddled together and twittered at the reference. "We must rebel." He rose his right arm upward. The left was, incongruously, still held aloft.

Loukia had decided to dress the *Evzones* in their traditional white skirts. She couldn't make the costumes, so she borrowed skirts from the village's girls. When the boys protested, she threatened to make them Turks.

"But how will we defeat them?" Taki said. "They are so many." He spoke down, toward the pompoms tied to his shoes. He gave every word equal weight and inflection, rendering the whole sentence meaningless.

"We have justice on our side," another *Evzone* said. His fellow rebels were standing in a row. Each stepped forward, one at a time, to deliver his own line.

"And the blessed Virgin Mary."

"And we are fighting for the great principles of our ancient civilization."

"Democracy and freedom."

"And we have knowledge of the mountains. So we will... um...we will use that—the knowledge of them...of the land."

The battle scene went more smoothly. The *Evzones* piled into a plane tree. At a signal given by the guerrilla leader, Vasilis, they all charged forward, attacking the table of Turks. They were careful not to knock over any of the glasses: the *taverna* owner had been reluctant to lend them.

Having slain most of the Turks with their fierce branch swords, the *Evzones* retreated to one side of the *platia*.

"That was a dirty attack," the head Turk said. Loukia had cast him for this role because he was her only friend with facial hair. "They did not fight fair. We will not fight fair, either. Come!" He swaggered to the girls. "Give us your children or we will kill all of you and burn down your houses and take your food."

Loukia broke from the group. "We will never surrender. If we cannot live with justice and freedom, then we will not live at all."

Papou Yiorgos listened to the children. His son was still in the hospital in Volos. Philip would survive, the doctors had said. He would be deformed and demented, but he would survive.

"Our men fight for justice. We will not betray them by living under the enemy. We will oppose them with our death."

The girls linked hands now, and Loukia led them in a dance. She had hoped her Papou would play violin for them, but he had declined, and her mother told her not to push. Instead, Loukia hummed the song, hitting all the beats. *Slow...fast, fast; slow...fast, fast; slow...fast, fast.* Everyone knew this rhythm; they'd danced to it at weddings and baptisms, here on the *platia*. *Slow*—the girls stepped heavily onto the ground, pulled downward. They recovered on the two fast beats, then succumbed again—*slow*—heavy. The better dancers could embody this conflict: this desire for the ground that's never quite allowed.

Loukia snaked the dance around the trees. The adults began to clap, in unison: *slow... fast, fast; slow... fast, fast.* Loukia mounted the low wall that bordered the *platia*. Her feet pranced in time to the clapping. Her torso was straight, her chest back, hips aligned. *Slow...fast, fast; slow...fast, fast; slow...* The other girls joined Loukia. Her arm lifted upward. The audience watched that long limb rise.

"Now," Loukia whispered to the other girls.

Without breaking the chain of hands, each girl jumped from the wall, as if off the cliffside, like the martyred women of Souli. They all lay together on the *platia*, believing they understood the beauty of tragic death.

Loukia looked at the sky and listened to the final scene, where the *Evzones* defeat the last of the Turks. Even though she'd written the play, Loukia couldn't follow the lines: the boys' voices seemed remote, the battle far away.

Twenty-One
April 1941

On April 6, 1941, Germany invaded Greece through Yugoslavia.

Within the month, Greek soldiers abandoned their weapons and fled, en masse; within the week, the Greek prime minister adjourned his final cabinet meeting and committed suicide; within three days, the king assumed power and fled with his government to Egypt; within two hours, the Nazis marched into Athens. The swastika was raised, immediately, over the Parthenon.

The news reached Zagora via the radio. The king addressed his people, praising their heroism against the Italians. He vowed that Free Greece would be resurrected, stronger than ever. Then he gave the airwaves to the Greek national anthem. That song looped back—fifty-eight seconds, a trumpet and drum and voice, fifty-eight seconds looping back for three hours, looping back fifty-eight seconds at a time, a short pause in between, while Taki moved closer to Papou on the couch, the afternoon progressing by fifty-eight seconds of trumpet and drum and voice and pause—fifty-eight seconds for three hours, looping, until silence.

"What is happening, Papou?" Taki grabbed his grandfather's arm. He squeezed, feeling the bone inside the aging muscle.

"The radio station isn't broadcasting anymore," he said. "The soldiers must have arrived."

Taki looked at his grandfather. "Is it over, Papou?" he asked. He blinked his Samsarelos eyes—brown and small, accepting of the world. These were different from Apostolides eyes, Papou Yiorgos thought: Apostolides eyes imposed their gaze on everything around them. "Is it—"

"No, Taki," Papou Yiorgos said. "It's not over." Papou didn't shut off the radio. He and Taki sat together, listening to the bristle of absence.

Part IV: Eight Seasons

Thessaloniki, Greece

Autumn 1941–Summer 1943

Twenty-Two
Autumn 1941

Mary sat at the edge of the bed, listening to Agamemnon wash himself in the bathroom. She'd served dinner early and sent everyone to sleep, arguing that the house wasn't properly proofed for the blackout order. Her bedroom window was the only one she'd covered in opaque drapes; she kept the gaslight on.

Agamemnon returned to the bedroom, a towel slung around his shoulders. He stroked the stubble on his cheek. "I'll have to shave in the morning," he said. "I couldn't turn on the light in there."

"You won't be here in the morning," Mary said. She looked straight ahead, her eyes level with the end of the towel on Agamemnon's chest. "You'll be on your way to Cairo. I've packed a bag for you."

Agamemnon sighed. "Who told you about that? Katarina?"

"You're not safe here. Go to Cairo. I want you to go."

Agamemnon had heard about that night's passage to Egypt. A merchant boat would be docked at a nearby harbour, according to one of his army colleagues. Two officers were due to crawl inside at 3 a.m. The boat would leave at dawn; there was room for two more men.

"Tell me: what kind of a man would I be if I left—"

"But, Agamemnon—"

"No. I'm not done." He stood tall before Mary; he forced her chin up with his finger. "What kind of a man would I be...to leave my family under occupation and sail off to Egypt."

"But—"

"*What* kind of a man?"

Mary pulled her face away, unwilling to be dominated. "What kind of men are your friends?" she demanded. "*They're* leaving *their* families."

Agamemnon smiled at his wife's ferocity. She'd been a girl when they'd met, just sixteen. Now she was thirty, the age he'd been when they'd married. Agamemnon tried to stroke her cheek, but she leaned away.

"Tell me, Agamemnon," she said, still defiant.

Agamemnon took her cheek in his hand, massaging it, hard. He scorned the notion of an exiled government of "Free Greece." Officers needed to see the situation on the ground, in the country, in order to respond properly. Reality would get skewed in the telling, across continents and the sea. Besides, he would never abandon his family to the enemy.

"They're cowards, Mary. And I made an oath."

"Agamemnon…"

"I made an oath to my country and my family. This is where I need to be."

"I don't want anything to happen to you."

He slid his hand from her cheek to the back of her neck and up, onto her scalp. He made a fist, intertwining her hair between his fingers. He pulled back with his hand; he wanted her, finally, to look at him. "This is where I need to be." Her eyes remained averted. He gripped tighter.

"Please, Agamemnon."

"No."

"Please go."

"I won't leave you."

She looked up, into his face.

"My beauty," he said. With his free hand, he touched his thumb to the corner of her eye, wicking away the tear. Gently, he dragged it down her neck, onto her chest. He did not ease his grip on her hair.

In the dark room next door, Taki could hear his parents' voices. He pulled his blanket over his head, turning their words into muddled sounds. He tried to think of a dream that might become real—vividly, perfectly real—when—if—he managed to fall asleep.

Agamemnon was not in bed when Mary awoke the following morning. "Agamemnon?" She sat up with a blood rush of understanding: he was gone. He'd slipped away in the middle of the night, just as she'd asked him to do. "Agamemnon," she whispered. Her skin still smelled of him.

Mary shut herself in the bathroom to wash before confronting her in-laws. She held a towel under the tap, watching it bloat in her hands. She couldn't imagine Egypt, except as dryness. She couldn't picture the streets, the trees, the colour of the light on houses. He was gone, into a blankness. Mary pushed the towel against her eyes, then down over her nose and mouth. She wasn't even sure Agamemnon would arrive safely. The trip across the Mediterranean was dangerous: she hadn't considered that risk the night before, when she'd packed his bag and urged him to leave. She hadn't envisioned the boat bobbing in the grey sea, with Agamemnon trapped inside. Maybe the Nazis were patrolling the water with warships, or submarines, or squadrons of airplanes; maybe a storm would rise up, pitching the tiny boat; maybe the merchant would get lost, or confused, or greedy. Maybe...

The sopping towel was heavy over Mary's mouth as she tried to breathe. She kept it that way, sucking in what little air she could, taking herself to the edge of panic. She hadn't said goodbye.

Taki heard his mother upstairs, running the water for an unusually long time. He was alone in the kitchen, arranging crumbs on his plate. He hoped she was in a good mood, otherwise she might mess up his plans for the day.

"Mama!" Taki said, greeting his mother with too much enthusiasm. "Mama, Dad says I can go to the villages with him today! Can I?"

"Oh, Taki," Mary sighed. "Your father isn't here. He went away...for work. For a while."

"No he didn't! He's downstairs! He didn't leave yet—he promised to take me!" Taki hopped out of his chair and ran to his father's office. For the past two months, Taki had begged his father to take him to the villages. Agamemnon had been travelling there frequently during the Nazi occupation. Instead of working at the army base, he would make the rounds of farmers' homes, treating the animals that lived out back.

"Mama!" Mary heard Taki's feet loud on the stairs. "Mama, he's still here!" Taki exclaimed. "He said I could go with him!"

Mary's head drooped down. "Taki, he's *gone*," she said, exasperated.

"Mama, he's not!"

"Taki," she warned, "I told you, he—"

"Mary..." Agamemnon's arms were crossed over his chest, his shoulder leaning against the doorframe. He hadn't yet shaven. "I snuck out of bed this morning. I didn't want to wake you." His voice was animal-deep compared to Taki's child whine.

"Agamemnon... I thought you'd—"

"I wouldn't leave you like that." Agamemnon smiled with one corner of his lips. "I made an oath, Mary. I won't break it." They held each other's gazes, communicating a complexity of feeling that a simple line of words would've flattened and destroyed.

"Can I go, Mama? Dad said I could.... Mama?"

Mary looked down at her boy. He was so eager and wanting, so ignorant of all that had happened the night before, and all that was happening now. She saw the arch of his eyebrows that had peaked in anticipation of her response. She marvelled at his lack of awareness—the purity of his innocence.

"Yes, Taki. If your father says it's okay."

"Dad?"

"You can come with me, Taki. As long as you're prepared to work, of course."

Taki became serious and settled, assuring his father that he would be a worthy apprentice.

"Good, Taki. And someday you'll be a worthy successor."

Taki nodded solemnly, but his father didn't notice.

"Get ready now, Taki," Agamemnon said, sending his boy off as he reached for his wife.

Taki dashed to the bedroom to change his clothes. He pulled on his shirt and shorts and scratchy white socks, rushing about to find his belt, bumping into his sister's bed. Loukia nuzzled her pillow; she sighed out a moan.

"Sorry," Taki whispered. He tiptoed out of the room, into the hall, where he heard his father's throaty laugh from the kitchen. Taki stopped: waited: unsure when to move.

"Is it morning?" Loukia asked.

Laspiti arrived within the hour to take Agamemnon and Taki to his village. The horse and cart manoeuvred around trolley cars and Nazi jeeps, toward the dirt road that led west, along the Thermaic Gulf, to the cluster of villages. Taki sat in the middle of the cart, between the two men.

"How's the harvest been?" Agamemnon asked, looking over Taki's head.

"It's been okay—only okay," Laspiti answered. "The weather's been cold, and some of the men are gone now." The long morning light shone off the crags of scar tissue on Laspiti's face. He scratched at a trickle of sweat that meandered down. Taki turned forward. "And some of the men who returned...well, some aren't really 'there' anymore. They're woozy, like the bees in October." Laspiti's hand swayed in front of Taki's face.

"That won't last," Agamemnon said. "They'll adjust. Life will make them adjust."

"Maybe."

The men spoke in detail about the villagers: which widows were coping, whose crops were failing, what gossip was working its way through the fields. Agamemnon listened to Laspiti's brief with the same attention he'd always given Maki's reports at army headquarters. They were, he knew, equally important.

Taki clutched his hands together between pressed knees. He was attempting to keep completely still, not letting himself get jostled left or right by the movement of the cart. The game was a test of himself; he thought he was losing.

"There's something else you should know," Laspiti said. "We got a visit from the Nazis yesterday."

"I'm not surprised. What did they want? Or let me put it this way: what did they *say* they wanted?"

Laspiti explained: apparently the Nazis had instituted a nationwide food-distribution system. They wanted to take the farmers' crops and seeds; they claimed they'd use the crops to feed the urban poor. "The urban poor!" Laspiti snorted. "More like their poor German bellies," he said—their voracious German hunger, their expanding German mouths, eating all of Europe, one village at a time, the bastards—he added.

Agamemnon paused, considering this information. "Tell me, Laspiti..."

Taki released his legs. His inner thighs felt rubbery from fatigue, though he hadn't moved at all.

"Tell me: what's the plan to stop the Nazis?"

Laspiti smiled. "I'll let you know on the ride home." The horse pulled the cart forward; the three listened to its progress.

"Hey, Taki," Laspiti said. "You have a sweetheart at school?" He nudged Taki with his elbow.

Taki looked up, startled.

"You sweet on someone?... Hey, Agamemnon, he's blushing! He's got a sweetheart—the blood never lies!"

Agamemnon chuckled. "The blood never lies, but sometimes it plays tricks."

"Yes. Sometimes," Laspiti sniffled. "Agamemnon, I should also tell you..."

"Did Constantia...?"

"She was partway through the second trimester this time."

Agamemnon sighed.

"Are we here?" Taki asked. He hadn't spoken since they'd left the kitchen at home.

The village was a grouping of homes built around the *platia*, with its church and cafés and *tavernas*. Nearby were the farmers' fields, separated by grey rock walls. The farm animals usually lived in the back of people's homes, in a single room filled with hay, the manure pile stored in one corner. The people lived in the front, where the bedding lay flat on the hard dirt floor, and a fireplace served as heater and stove. Chairs were always kept on the porches, which were covered by a trellis of grapevines.

Agamemnon went to nine homes that day. With every family he visited, he accrued more admirers. By the time he examined the last animal of the day, two dozen people had flocked around him. They all came, ignoring their fields and homes, to watch him work. Because he was special. He—a city man, an educated man, an officer of the Greek army; he with lovely hands and pale skin, with knowledge and refinement—he was an event in their midst.

"How long has the animal been lethargic?" Agamemnon asked the farmer. He stroked the horse's neck.

"About four weeks, doctor."

Agamemnon nodded and spoke to the horse. "Let's see what's going on, old man," he said. He pulled down the animal's lower eyelid and examined the mucus membrane. Taki watched from the edge of the gathered villagers.

"That looks okay," Agamemnon said, sliding his hand down the horse's muzzle. He slipped his fingers inside the animal's mouth, between the lower lip and gums. "How's its appetite?" He swiped his fingers across the warm tissues of the mouth.

"Not very good."

"Mm-hm." Agamemnon rubbed the saliva between his thumb and forefingers. He brought the triad to his nose and smelled his fingertips. "Okay," he said. He put his hand onto the horse's neck again. Without ever breaking contact, he walked around the animal. He squatted, then pushed with the heel of his hand into the horse's belly. His shoulder rotated as he probed, sensing the shape of the organs, checking for tumors or distension, for the way the body pushed back.

"Taki, bring me the towel," he said. Taki stepped past the group of villagers, into the circular space where his father stood. "Come, I want you to listen." Agamemnon draped the towel over the horse's rib cage. He then put his hand on Taki's slight back, just below the neck.

Taki felt that touch as heat.

"Like this. Put your palm to the chest. Put your ear next to it. Listen."

Taki bent awkwardly toward the animal. Sounds from the outside were smothered at first. He heard nothing but the wind trapped in his ear.

"Just relax, Taki. Listen for a heartbeat." Agamemnon's hand pulsed on his son's back, finding the blood rhythm of a one-thousand-pound creature. "Listen."

Taki strained to hear.

"Relax," his father repeated.

Taki shut his eyes in frustration. He thought he might lie. He could lift up his face and declare that he'd heard it: the heartbeat, strong and sure.

"Relax, Taki."

The horse tossed its head. Taki heard a rub and shift of hair and breath. He heard those sounds echo and dissolve, as if in a tunnel, from which he now heard something new: a thumping, low and contained. He listened. The sound grew—not louder, but more distinct, more palpable, its contours more clear.

"Good, Taki," Agamemnon said. "You've found it."

Taki turned abruptly toward his father. "How did you know?"

Agamemnon smiled. "Tell me, Taki," he answered. "What did you just learn?"

"I learned... I..."

"You heard the heartbeat. It was even, right?"

"Right."

"And you heard it with your ear, yes? And you felt it with your hand?"

"Yes."

Agamemnon now enumerated all the senses. With each one, he touched a part of Taki's face. His fingers were not delicate on Taki's lips and eyes, his nose and ears and cheek. This touch was businesslike, meant to emphasize his point: these senses were the most important tools a veterinarian could possess. Use them, the touch seemed to say. Lean in, listen, grab, see, smell, taste: use them. "Do you understand, Taki? You learn to feel an animal's muscle tense up or relax. You learn to detect the slight variations of the body. You anticipate its moves. You surmise its injuries."

"I understand, Dad," Taki said. He did, he thought. He *did* understand all of those words. "But how could you tell that I heard the heartbeat?" he asked.

Agamemnon tapped his son's ear in response. "Listen," he said. Then he turned to give his diagnosis.

Agamemnon dispensed medicine—some tincture to ease the horse's indigestion—and the men discussed the prognosis, which was good. The harvest would go faster now.

"But what difference will it make," the farmer said. "Those parasites—the Nazis—they'll take all my crops anyway." He looked directly at Agamemnon. "Don't you think, doctor?"

Agamemnon shrugged. "Maybe not," he said. He turned toward the circle of villagers. "Tell me," he continued. "That old house behind the *platia*...? Does it still have the storage room in the basement? The one that's hidden?"

Twenty-Three
Winter 1941

By the beginning of winter, the Nazis had requisitioned dozens of Thessaloniki's buildings to billet their army. Gondicas's school was converted into barracks, as were the two large homes bordering the back of Taki's house. These homes were owned by Jewish families; they—the spinning girl and her parents, brothers, grandparents (four)—were living with relatives now, though they'd all be sent to the ghetto soon. Taki hadn't seen them go.

Gondicas refused to close his school when the Germans overtook his building. Within the month, he'd rearranged his house so he could teach from his bedroom. He'd amalgamated three classes into one, since his student body was rapidly dwindling: the Jewish kids were penned in the ghetto near the railroad station; several boys had gotten jobs, replacing their dead or injured fathers as the families' wage earners; one girl had died of tuberculosis. Then there was Panayiotis Panayiotidis, the teenager whose father owned the yogourt shop. Panayiotis had written an impassioned letter to Gondicas, urging him to alter his teaching philosophy: in this era of war, he argued, the Spartan focus on physical strength and acumen was more important than the Athenian ideal of intellectual dexterity. Athenians played with the hand and mind, using ideas as their adult toys; Spartans, by contrast, used their feet and bodies to stay responsive to the real world. This, the boy wrote, using a crescendo of rather heroic prose, was the ancient model that Gondicas should follow as the continent was consumed by conflagration.

Gondicas filed the letter away. Panayiotis' ability to write it, he thought, was evidence that his school's pedagogical techniques were working beautifully.

Gondicas reluctantly fired his staff and began teaching the single remaining class himself. He didn't trust anyone else to manage a room with students aged eight to seventeen. Most teachers would've catered to the younger kids; by contrast, Gondicas wrote his curriculum for the older ones. The others would catch on, he decided.

"Today we start preparatory work for the *Odyssey*," Gondicas said, standing at the blackboard. He'd removed his personal photographs and furniture, replacing them with the school's maps and desks. In the new space, these objects seemed small and shabby—diminished without actually changing. "This is one of the five works that everyone must read before he dies." Nikos Hadzis rolled his eyes. Gondicas often uttered that phrase; he never identified the other four works.

"The *Odyssey* is a series of episodes in Odysseus's journey from the conquered city of Troy to his home in Ithaca.... By the way," he said, his hands clasped, "the older students will be assigned one episode of the *Odyssey* to examine as a requirement for graduation." Several students picked up their pencils. "So," Gondicas continued. "The history of the book itself."

Taki was curved over his desk, his face close to his notebook as he scribbled away.

"This poem was not meant to be read as a book. It was a story told orally. As such," Gondicas continued, pacing in front of the class, "it changed according to the teller of the tale."

Taki tried to capture Gondicas's exact words, but he couldn't keep up. He was quickly lost, the meaning detached from the words he recorded. His other teacher hadn't been this difficult; his other teacher had emphasized penmanship and verb tense. Taki snuck a look to his left. He could smell his nervous sweat through his shirt.

"Homer was merely the first to write the stories down. As such, *his* version is *the* version."

Dimitra sat at the desk beside Taki. She was staring at Gondicas; her pencil rested on her notebook. She twirled a loose strand of hair around her finger. Taki looked at his notebook, then back to the girl, whose writing hand was still on her hair. She wasn't taking notes! He looked down again:

Poem—story
oral—change—teller—version—version

"Subtle variations, incisive meanings that changed according to audience and storyteller—all are lost in the service of this one version." Gondicas paused in his pacing and raised his finger into the air. "It is the tragedy," he intoned, jabbing his finger, "the tragedy of the written word. To get this work of art, we must end its evolution. We must deny the complexities of its past, and seal it from whatever future interpretations it might possibly have developed." He resumed his pacing.

Subtle var—meaning lost—tragedy
written—
art end no past, seal future—what
possible

Gondicas began, then, with the first story of the book.

Classes ended with the tinkling of a little brass bell. Gondicas's mother stepped into the doorway. "Classes are done for the day," she sang. She'd assumed the role of timekeeper ever since the school had moved into her house. She seemed cheerful about interrupting her son. "Time to play, children."

The students looked expectantly to Gondicas, their legs prepped to stand. "We aren't done with the lesson."

"Oh, my boy," Gondicas's mother said. "It's time for the children to play."

Nikos was the first to leave. When his lanky body disappeared out the door, all the other kids sprang up. Gondicas pressed his fingertips onto his desk, locking himself there, leaning forward, muscles taut. These new circumstances were no good, he thought, watching the students leave. The school's relocation to his home had undercut his authority. Even Aliki was going.

"Tomorrow we'll continue with the *Odyssey*," Gondicas called. "Bring sharp pencils!"

His mother rang the bell again. "Be careful in the backyard, children," she said. "They're doing some work back there."

"*Several* sharp pencils."

"Goodbye, Mrs. Gondicas," Taki said.

The woman grasped his chin. Her hand was cold, but not like the chill of his grandmother's touch; this cold was like a stream, alive. "You are so serious, little one." Taki tried to look aside, embarrassed at being singled out. "I understand. There's a lot to be serious about, isn't there, Taki Apostolides?"

"Yes, Mrs. Gondicas."

She smiled at him and pinched his chin before letting him out the door.

Taki joined the other students in Gondicas's backyard, where they gathered around a room-sized trench. The mound of freshly dug dirt was taller than some of the kids. "Another bomb shelter?" Taki asked.

"I guess so." Nikos peered into the hole. The rectangular den was connected to a narrow channel that zigzagged sharply. Gondicas had designed the shelter. The angled channel was meant to stop shrapnel from flying inside; the top and sides would be framed in concrete.

"Wanna play soccer?" Taki asked his friends. He couldn't be near that bomb shelter right now. Its empty pit held too many implications.

"Girls against boys," Nikos said.

"No way!" Loukia laughed, her shoulder tilting to her ear at the silliness of the suggestion. Nikos wasn't prepared for her absolute cuteness.

"I'll be on Taki's team," Dimitra declared.

"Okay," Nikos said, his voice hoarse.

The kids slipped through the hedges, to the Apostolides' backyard. Taki set down some jackets as goalposts. He stepped back, assessing the size of the proposed goal; he looked up: a man was smiling at him—a German soldier, in full uniform, who stood on the rooftop of the neighbour's home, along with four others. That Nazi nodded, specifically to Taki. He'd noted Taki there, in the yard, individually, an individual. Taki had been spotted.

"The goal is too narrow," Dimitra said, adjusting one of the jackets.

"Sorry." The word came out quiet.

For the first while, the game had no momentum, especially since Loukia kept kicking the ball into the bushes. The kids were lucky to complete any plays at all.

"I'm open!" Dimitra called. Taki passed her the ball. She dribbled easily around Loukia. Nikos now stood between her and the goal. He manoeuvred to cut her off. She dribbled close, then faked to the right. Her shirt lifted up as she ran; Taki saw the dark oval of her belly button, the white flash of skin. She ran around Nikos and tapped the ball into the goal.

"Score!" Dimitra slapped Taki's hand. Strands of hair had fallen out of her ponytail, onto her face. "Good pass, Taki!" Her front teeth overlapped each other.

"Good shot—really!"

If Taki had looked closely enough, he would've seen that Dimitra's eyes were dark green and flecked with the same brown as her hair. That symmetry lent her face a calm aspect, but only until she smiled: then her crooked teeth gave the impression of whimsy.

"All right, Loukia, let's get it back," Nikos chanted. "Let's get it back!"

They never did: Dimitra scored three more times, even though she was trying to go easy on Loukia. After her fourth goal, the kids heard some laughter, directed down at them. Spiros was smoking on his balcony.

"Sorry, kids, but she's got you beat!" he called. He'd survived the war against Italy with no physical injuries. He looked the same, except, perhaps, that he wore his moustache a bit thicker. "You boys just can't keep up." He took a drag on his cigarette, his chest expanding languorously. "You better watch out for her when she's older," he said, laughing as he exhaled.

"Hi, Spiros!" Loukia said, unhappy about being ignored. "How are you?"

"Just fine, Loukia." He liked female attention, even if it was from a girl. He chuckled. "Just fine."

Loukia strode to the bench beneath the fig tree: she was done with the game. Nikos trotted behind. As he sat on the bench beside Loukia, his knee bumped into hers. He felt a buzz of shock zip through his knee bone, all the way up. Loukia tossed her hair off her face and chest. "I got very hot," she said. "Very sweaty."

"Yes?" Nikos responded.

Dimitra kept dribbling around the yard, averting imaginary defencemen. Taki observed her control of the ball, the movement of her muscle. He watched. Then he looked away.

The workmen in Gondicas's yard had finished digging the trench. One man, an unemployed army veteran, was mixing some wet concrete in a shallow wooden box, dragging the rake toward himself, repeatedly. The sweat from the day's labour had plastered his shirt to his skin, moulding to the shape of his back.

"Is it ready?" the other workman asked.

"Almost."

The two men would pour the concrete, forming the shelter's walls, once it was mixed to the right consistency: the pebbled sealant had to be gloppy, but not so dense that it couldn't give a bit, breathe a bit, even when hardened and set in place.

On the southern border of the Apostolides' property, the German soldiers were hammering wooden planks onto the rooftops, creating a walkway between the houses. Taki couldn't figure out the function of the walkway. But he sensed they were linked: the large hole dug in the dirt, and the platform high above the ground. They were linked, and he was in the middle.

"Taki!" Mary stood in the doorway, one hand upraised. "Taki, I need you to get the bread." She waved the ration card in the air. "Now."

"Can I walk Dimitra home?" Taki asked.

"Do you want to eat over the next three days?"

"Yes."

"Then no."

Dimitra abandoned the ball and started to leave.

"And don't go near *anyone*, Taki. Do you understand?" Mary said. "Don't touch *anyone*."

"Yes, Mama," he said, taking the card from his mother.

"And go straight to the bakery before they run out."

"Yes, Mama."

Mary grabbed Taki's wrist as he turned to go. Her hunger was now felt in her nerves, not her belly. "Don't just say, 'Yes Mama, yes Mama,'" she said, using a high-pitched, pathetic voice. "Do—you—understand...."

"Yes, Mama."

She shoved him, as if she couldn't stand to look at him anymore.

"I understand," he called back, running through the laneway. He pumped his legs, hoping to catch up to Dimitra. He'd barely left the gate when he bumped into the body.

"Excuse me," the woman said. She wore a black wool coat whose smooth buttons were made of bone. On her chest was a bright yellow star.

Taki backed away. "I'm sorry, I..."

"It was my fault," the woman said, her accent distinct. This was Taki's former neighbour.

"No. Really, it wasn't. It..." Taki sidled past her, contracting the muscles of his gut, making himself as thin as possible. "It..."

Dimitra was up ahead. Taki walked faster, pushed and pulled in the same direction. He heard a garbage cart lag behind him. The cart's horse trudged forward—the lapse long between each step, the load heavy inside the hold. The wheels were metal, larger than the pre-war wooden ones. They scraped against the cobblestones of the street. Their sound sparked outward.

"Dimitra!" Taki called.

One Nazi met another on the opposite side of the street. They greeted each other, guttural. Taki tried to tell if they were the men who'd recognized him, if they knew where he lived. He looked without looking, trying to tell—to notice without being noticed. He looked, and both men gestured at once: in a flash, their arms struck upward, sending a bolt of lightning from their fingertips.

Taki tripped forward. The garbage cart passed him. Its hold cast a shadow on the sidewalk. Dimitra was gone, having turned toward home. Taki said goodbye to her in his mind.

The bread line, luckily, was short, bending around only one corner. Taki tapped his feet—step-and-tap...left-to-right...side-to-side—to keep some sense of time and progress as he waited. Another garbage cart ground along the street. The bread line moved past the newsagent's shop, where the owner's son was stacking Nazi-approved papers on some racks. His voice box slid up and down his neck continuously as he worked.

"Lies... Fascist lies... Just a matter of time," he muttered. He stood straight and stretched his back. His eyes stopped on Taki, as if caught on barbed wire. He grinned. "It's just a matter of time," he said.

Taki took two steps forward, cramming closer to the person ahead of him.

"Can you spare some cigarettes?" a man asked. He was sitting on the sidewalk, leaning against an abandoned storefront. The bread line bulged around him and his family.

On the wall behind him, the Nazis had plastered a propaganda poster. They'd used all the available space: four posters across, three posters down, a square of saturated colour. The image featured a Nazi foot marching forward, the treaded black sole large in the centre. With four across and three down—the picture repeated, abutted—Taki swore he saw that boot move, crushing the little city below.

"Some food?" the man asked. His pants were dirty and threadbare. He'd wrapped an intricately knit scarf around his neck, but he wore no coat. "Food? For me or my kid? Any food?"

The kid's head was closely shaven. He curled against his mother, who sifted through the stubble, picking out lice. He shivered beneath his father's coat.

"Can you spare some food?" the man chanted. "For my kid? Any food?"

The man reached his hand upward. Taki watched the red, chafed palm get closer to him, the arm uncoiling. "No," Taki said, retracting his chin and shoulders. "I have nothing." He stepped back, staring at the hand. "I have nothing," he repeated, though the man was already begging from someone else.

"Cigarettes? Food? For me or—"

"Out! We're all outta bread!" the baker's wife called, ringing a cowbell. "Come back tomorrow!" The bell made the boy cover his ears.

"Cigarettes? Food? For my kid?"

Back in New York, Stevie was learning to smoke his first cigarette. Those initial drags were inadequate: he drew the harsh grey air only into his mouth, letting it swirl around his teeth and tongue. The motion was sexy, but otherwise the whole endeavour was unspectacular.

Stevie looked around the dark football field, nervous. The older boy, soon to be drafted, made a joke. Stevie laughed and made some remark; as the two boys laughed, alone on the deserted football field, Stevie drew again. This time his throat was open, allowing the smoke to enter his body. Now he felt that exquisite lightness—the lightness of everything leaving.

Twenty-Four
Spring 1941

The wildflowers had begun to bloom along the side of the road. The Nazis were pushing through North Africa, the Americans were landing in Europe, and London was soldiering on despite aerial attacks. The Greek government-in-exile was trying to keep busy, though it couldn't actually implement policy from its well-appointed headquarters in Cairo. Meanwhile, Greek communist leaders formed guerrilla groups in the mountains throughout Greece. The groups, united in the movement called EAM/ELAS, declared that they had two goals: to fight the Axis occupiers, and to build a democratic government once the occupation was over. Planting season had arrived in the villages.

"Have you heard about the Americans? Are they going to win the war for us?" a farmer asked. He and the others stood in a circle around Agamemnon and the horse. Their drawstring pants and buttoned shirts stank from their days in the fields; their sweat had soaked their shirts, then evaporated, leaving only an odour that became sharper as the days passed. The villagers had gathered on a patch of grass outside the barn. The manure pile was alive with flies.

"I don't think it will be that simple," Agamemnon said. He bent to examine the horse's injury. His fingers rolled, percussive, up the swollen leg. When he reached one particular spot, the animal swung its neck and bellowed. "It's okay," Agamemnon commanded. He eased a finger back and forth above the ankle joint, feeling the fluid that pooled inside the tissue.

"How long has the animal been limping?" he asked the farmer.

"Two days, doctor. Two or three."

"And was there a specific injury—a blow or a twist?"

"Not that I know of. There might have been, of course."

"Of course."

Taki stood beside his father, unseen in the centre of everything.

"Taki," Agamemnon said. "I need you to build a fire. Get the matches from my bag. The rod, too."

Agamemnon had explained this procedure to Taki once before: the rod would be held over a fire until it became sufficiently hot, at which point it would be placed directly on the horse's injured limb. The rod would then bring heat, which would bring blood, which would remove the toxins that caused the limp, in theory.

"It'll take a moment before we begin," Agamemnon told the farmer.

Taki searched the ground for dry sticks.

"What do you think of this EAM/ELAS, doctor?" one villager asked. "I hear they want to attack the Nazis. They say we can be proud again."

Agamemnon had known this farmer since the mid-1930s. He'd delivered his mare's foal, and the foal borne by that mare years later. "I don't think it's a question of 'pride against the Nazis.'"

"But they blew up a road, not far from here. And the Nazis, they couldn't move their trucks for hours. The trucks just sat there—these huge machines stopped by one little bomb! Just one little thing! That's all we have—one little thing. But we're *smart*," the farmer said, tapping his temple. "The Greeks are *smart*. We stopped them with *nothing*. That takes a lot of guts—real manliness."

Agamemnon shrugged. "I don't know. It was certainly very showy." He was washing his hands in the fountain, seemingly indifferent to this conversation.

"I guess it's showy," the farmer said. "But what a show!" He looked around for confirmation, nodding his head to his fellow villagers. "A good show, wasn't it?"

Agamemnon coughed two times, precisely.

Taki had been taught how to build a fire in the Boy Scouts. He arranged the sticks in a pyramid, leaving a hatching of holes. A fire needs air—it breathes air like a person, the Boy Scouts' leader had said. He'd been killed at Koritsa; his Boy Scout troop hadn't reassembled. Taki lit the fire.

"The trucks were there for *hours.*"

"Hours. Interesting. Tell me, did you have a plan for responding to the attack, assuming the Nazis had come to the village? Assuming they'd asked for the names of the men who'd set the bomb?"

"No, but..." The man puffed up his cheeks, then popped the air out audibly. "I mean, the men weren't *from* this village."

"Do you think the Nazis care?"

"I guess not, but—"

"So what was the plan?"

A woman waved her arm now, the muscle stringy on the bone. "I heard they shot eight men in Klissoura," she said. "Innocent men, with children! Shot them in the *platia*—boom!" She clapped her hands together—*boom*—a brisk slap, quick and done.

Agamemnon began to cleanse the horse's leg with alcohol. He glanced at the villagers as they argued. Some of them said the Greeks would betray their heritage if they did nothing against the Axis. "And not just the ancients! But the fallen heroes of Epirus, too!" one said. "May they rest in peace," he added. Several people made the sign of the cross.

"There won't be any peace if we kill a Nazi soldier!" a woman responded, her voice nasal and piercing.

"She's right. Did you hear about the new law? The Nazis said they'll—"

The villagers shouted across the circle at each other, their voices intersecting. Agamemnon let them yell. He was the only one who was truly listening, hearing the themes and perspectives that got tangled in the confusion of this war.

"Doctor," one man called. "Doctor, what do *you* think we should do?"

"What should we do?" Agamemnon said. He'd finished arranging his tools on a tray, placing scalpels and razors in two straight rows. "We should strengthen our communities—take care of our own. Keep ourselves fed, educated. And we should leave the Germans alone—they won't be here forever. And *we* can't defeat them by ourselves. This war is happening all over the world. A few of us here—we can't defeat them."

A young man sniggered. He wore his beard long, his hair curly on his forehead. Agamemnon didn't recognize him. He paused, assessing. He then chose a razor and shaved the hair off the horse's ankle, running the blade upward to reveal the stark-white skin, lacking pigment. "Tell me," he said, glancing back at the man. "Tell me: what do you think we should do?"

"We should attack them," the man said, without hesitation. "We can't defeat the Germans...you're right about that. But we *can* slow them down. We can cost them money." He brushed his hair off his face. "We can kill some." Along his forehead was a white scar, the dead skin knitted together in an uneven seam. The wound had not been clean: it had been the result of a sudden accident, Agamemnon thought, or a careful calculation.

"We can kill some Germans, true," Agamemnon responded. "And then they'll kill some of us."

"It's a war. People die in wars."

Agamemnon wiped the blade on his thigh, removing the horse's hairs. "What's your name?" he asked.

"Aleko Alexiou."

Agamemnon nodded. This was the son of a local farmer, the boy who'd been imprisoned for his communist activities years earlier.

"And what's yours?" Aleko asked.

Agamemnon laid the razor on the tray. "I'm Dr. Agamemnon Apostolides."

"Yes," Aleko said. "I've heard of you."

By now, the rod had absorbed the flame into itself, assuming its colour and lustre. Taki watched the red glow seep up the rod.

"I've treated your father's animals," Agamemnon replied.

Aleko shook his head, not breaking his gaze. "No. That's not how I know your name."

Agamemnon stepped from the circle of villagers, their bodies stiffened and silent. He put his hand flat on Taki's shoulder. The boy twitched. "Is the rod ready?"

"I think it might be."

"What you 'think' is not pertinent here. I asked whether the rod was ready."

Taki felt the warmth seep up. He did not respond.

"Excuse me," Agamemnon said, taking the rod from his son and passing beside Aleko. "I must attend to the mare now."

Sheepish, Taki followed his father into the circle. Once they were in the proper position, Agamemnon brought the rod, gently, to the horse's flesh. The mare bellowed, a low moan resonating in the hollows of its chest and throat. Taki watched the flesh burn. He could hear the sizzle on the leg. The horse's front leg locked, making the animal stumble. "Pull its head down, get some air into it," Agamemnon said.

The farmer pulled on the bridle; the horse's neck plunged. The smell of singed muscle entered the cavities of Taki's head. The horse's eyes bulged, the whites shot through with red.

"Good," Agamemnon said. "This is good. We're almost done." Agamemnon pulled the rod away. The ankle was pulpy.

Taki's gut heaved. The vomit rose into his mouth, but he forced it back. It slid, grainy, down his throat.

"Bandage, Taki... Now."

Taki handed the white roll of cloth to his father and relieved him of the rod. The tip was no longer bright; bits of skin and flesh clung to it, dulling the glow. Agamemnon wound the bandage around the meat-exposed leg. "Will she recover?" the farmer asked. He paced in front of the animal.

"We'll see," Agamemnon said, ripping the cloth and tying it securely. "These injuries...they're difficult to treat completely."

The farmer nodded, concerned. The horse was all he had to till the fields, thresh the wheat, bring the harvest to market. "What do I owe you?" His voice wavered.

Agamemnon shook his head. He didn't require payment in cash. He wanted, instead, to demonstrate his generosity in public. He, a city man, an educated man, an officer of the Greek army... "You can pay me later," he said. "Once that mare brings in your harvest."

"But—"

"It's okay. These are unusual times."

"Yes, they are," Aleko said.

Agamemnon sighed. "Would you care to discuss this further?" he asked. "Over a drink, perhaps?"

"No," Aleko replied. "No, Dr. Agamemnon Apostolides. No—I'm expected elsewhere."

Taki watched Aleko break from the circle and swagger toward the *platia*.

"Well," Agamemnon said. His voice seemed steady, despite the day's procedures. "If anyone else wants to discuss this further, I will certainly remain. My other obligations can wait."

"I have a question," one man said. The circle collapsed together. They headed toward the verandah, where the farmer's wife had placed some olives, bread and ouzo. "Doctor, a document was left on the church door—a charter of some kind. Can you read it to us? Some of the language is—"

Taki did not join the adults. He remained in the back of the barn. He sat on the ground beside a patch of thyme. With his thumbnail, he scraped along a stem, removing dozens of tiny leaves. He brought his fingers to his nose, rubbing until the plant's tissue tore. He breathed in, his lungs expanding. But even this green pungency couldn't strip the smell of the mare from his head.

Mary was rolling out dough, thin, across the kitchen table. She was improvising a cracker recipe, using water instead of oil. "Did you get anything from the villages yesterday?" she called to Agamemnon. "Any little something?" She wiped her hands on a tea towel, leaving little dough balls caught in the fabric. She considered adding them to the cracker pan, but rejected the idea.

"They gave me some olives and figs. They're in the basement."

"Excellent," Mary said to herself. The evening was coming together nicely. In a few hours, Agamemnon's army friends would arrive for their monthly poker night. They'd resumed these nights that winter, despite the risk involved in violating the Nazis' curfew. "I'll just get those olives," she said, heading toward the basement through the parlour.

Agamemnon was tending to the fire in the wood-burning stove. He was crouched down, adjusting the logs with a long iron poker whose tip was shaped into a slim arrow. Mary brushed her fingers along his shoulders on the way past. She heard Yiayia Loukia harrumph in disapproval.

"And the figs, too," Mary added, winking at Agamemnon. He watched her turn the curve into the hallway, down the stairs. Her hand lingered on the doorframe before sliding away.

Mary was inordinately excited about the poker night. She hadn't entertained anyone in almost two years. She hummed as she descended the stairs. She would put the olives in the blue serving bowls, she decided, atop a silver platter for the crackers and figs. The crackers would be dry but they'd present well beside the olives. She wished she had cheese. She heard footsteps on the stairs.

"Did you find everything?" Agamemnon asked.

"Yes," she said. "Not a problem." She was bending over the basket from the village. Agamemnon put his hands onto her back, his thumbs pushing against the bands of muscle beside her spine. "You've gotten strong these last few years," he said.

"Out of necessity."

His hands worked up her spine. Her chest rose to his touch, her back arching. Agamemnon massaged her shoulders, the base of her neck.

"This is like before," she said. "Before the war and…" She turned to face Agamemnon.

"It will be like this again," he said. "And then we'll complain of being bored."

"I promise I will *never* complain of being bored.…"

"I'll hold you to that," he said, smiling. His eyes seemed retired, his face weary.

Mary kissed her husband with an urgency that surprised them both.

"Now," Agamemnon said, stepping back, "let's prepare for the guests. I'll begin by getting my parents away from the parlour." He strode up the stairs, aware that Mary was watching him.

The men arrived one at a time, according to a prearranged plan. First came Maki, through an unlocked window in Agamemnon's office. He crept up the stairs, startling Mary as she snuck an olive.

"Caught you," he said, poking her in the ribs, ruining the taste in her mouth.

"Maki," she said. "So good to see you again." Maki smiled through this thick moustache and beard.

Next came Costa. Katarina came with him, an unexpected treat for Mary. Last to arrive was Yianni, through the back door. Maki had decided to invite him into their intimate circle, glad to replace an officer who had fled to Cairo.

"There are too many women in here," Maki asserted. "Give me the cards, Agamemnon. Let's get started."

Mary took Katarina's hand. "Was it frightening?" she asked as they entered the kitchen. "To be out after curfew? Were you afraid?"

"Oh, Mary, it was beautiful!" Katarina replied. "The whole city was dark, and quiet. We were like spies!" She and Costa had walked on side streets and alleyways; they'd pressed themselves against stone walls, then dashed across the open road, to the next hidden corner. They hadn't encountered any Nazi patrols, Katarina said, but they'd heard an engine nearby, and once Costa thought he saw the glow of a cigarette. Already, the journey had become a story to her, divorced from any real danger.

"And now," Katarina said, "I think I'd like a drink!"

The women giggled, and Mary poured some ouzo.

"To invisibility," Katarina said in a toast.

The women clinked glasses.

"To the day when invisibility doesn't matter," Mary replied.

The men played two quick rounds of poker. The first round had gone to Maki, the second to Agamemnon. The third round was underway. The food was gone, the ouzo bottle emptying. Maki reordered his cards. These shifts were done slowly, with pauses between the movements; he wanted to be sure those around the table would notice. "Did you hear about EAM/ELAS?" he asked, without looking up.

Costa and Yianni shared what they had learned about the new guerrilla groups. Their information conflicted somewhat. Costa had heard that EAM/ELAS was funded by the Soviets; Yianni heard they received arms from the British. Costa said they were sabotaging Axis outposts; Yianni learned they had established schools and courts in the villages.

"Well, that's all very interesting," Maki said, impatient. "But let me tell you something: EAM/ELAS is the Communist Party, pure and simple. They're the communists, same as before the war. They don't give a shit about the Germans. They care about *after* the Germans are gone."

Costa folded.

Agamemnon considered his move. "Okay. But according to EAM's charter—"

"Where did you read their charter?" Yianni asked.

"Wait—let me finish.... According to the charter, EAM is against the *Axis*, not the king and his government. The charter says they want democratic elections after the war."

Maki guffawed and downed his ouzo, slamming his glass onto the table. He poured himself another.

Agamemnon turned to Yianni. "And in answer to your question, I read it in the villages. Yesterday, in fact." Agamemnon poured himself a glass, then tipped the bottle toward Costa and Yianni in turn, questioning if they wanted more. Both indicated that they did. "They're serious, this EAM."

"Do you believe them? Do you believe their charter—that they're against the Axis only?" Yianni asked.

Agamemnon kept his cards and tossed some coins into the pot. "I didn't say that. What I believe," he said, "is that they're organized. What I *know* is that we're not. *We* are in Egypt." He took a sip of ouzo. "Has anyone heard anything from Egypt, by the way?"

"No," Costa said. "Nothing. In sixteen months, nothing."

"And you can bet they haven't heard anything about any charter," Agamemnon said. He tapped the bottom of his glass against the table, impatient, then took a deeper drink. "Tell me, officers," Agamemnon continued. "I've been wondering... My contacts in the villages have been wondering, too. Tell me: what are *we* going to do about this situation?"

Yianni sighed, then folded.

"Agamemnon," Maki said, "you ask a very good question."

Without hesitating, he tossed in more coins. Maki's confidence was hard to read. He might be bluffing—he'd always been cavalier about risk. Then again, he was also precise in his calculations, conscious of the razor-thin opening of true opportunity.

Agamemnon swirled his empty glass. He glanced toward the kitchen. Mary and Katarina were sitting at the table, talking. He could see Mary's foot wrapped around the leg of her chair. He watched her laugh. Mary had lost too much weight: she'd been giving her bread to the children and in-laws, foregoing whatever cheese they could buy. He didn't want her body disappearing anymore. Agamemnon picked two coins from his dwindling stash and placed them into the centre pile. He should've folded.

"Let's see what you're holding, Officer Apostolides," Maki said. He spit an olive pit into his fist, having sucked off the last of its meat. He tossed it into the blue bowl, where it clung to the other pits already gathered.

He and Agamemnon laid down their hands.

"You are too obvious, Agamemnon," Maki said, drawing the money toward himself. "An okay hand—that's all you had." He organized his coins into stacks, ostentatiously arranging each one. "Let me give you a piece of advice," he added. "You checked with your wife for approval. Never do that, my friend."

By the end of spring, these monthly gatherings had shifted in focus and intent: without explicit planning, the poker nights had become meetings of a clandestine political cell. The four men decided they would shore up support for the Greek government-in-exile, including the king. Agamemnon and Costa would lead a propaganda effort, starting with their clients; Yianni would locate sympathetic printers who might reproduce some pamphlets; Maki would try to contact the British and the exiled Greek government in Cairo. The four officers didn't give their group a title: their efforts didn't require a name to define them. They were simply Greeks talking with Greeks, communicating their vision for a stronger nation, one man to another.

That's all: just words.

Twenty-Five
Summer 1942

Loukia spotted the bell tower, which was taller than most on Mount Pelion. "Almost there!" she said.

This church was in the village just east of Zagora. Its bell tower had become a landmark on the family's summer journey up the mountain. The sight unfailingly stirred them from their travel-induced torpor.

Loukia raised her arms above her head, her palms flat to the sky. "I can't wait to go swimming," she said. "I can't wait!"

Taki pushed his arms down, his muscles quivering in a stretch. "Mama," he said, "will Philip be in Zagora?"

"Yes." Mary unfastened her purse and rummaged around.

"Is he still sick?"

"No." She snapped her purse shut without removing anything. "And don't make any comments about it."

Mary ordered the driver to stop where the dirt road curved in front of her parents' house. Papou Yiorgos Samsarelos trotted down the well-worn path from the verandah. "I'm sorry, but you must be the wrong family," he said. "You're not my grandkids... you're much too big to be *my* grandkids."

"No, Papou! It's us!" Taki bounced in his seat. Mary indulged her father with a smile.

"Taki, I was going to give you a butter cookie," Papou Yiorgos said, "but maybe you're too big for that...."

"I'm not, Papou! Please!"

"Do I get one, too?" Loukia asked. She stepped off the cart, into a curtsy.

"Well..."

"Is it really a real *koulouri*?" Taki asked. He felt his mouth fill with saliva. "Do you really have one?"

Papou Yiorgos winked at Mary. He hadn't shaved yet that morning; his cheeks were coarse with short grey hairs. Those hairs...they were the reason his face was drained of colour, Mary told herself.

Papou Yiorgos unwrapped some brown paper, in which he held two butter cookies. He gave one to each of the children.

"Thank you," Taki said with a reverence he'd never felt in church. The dough had been rolled into two fat bands, then twisted into a braid. The top was coloured a warm brown; lines of shiny coating had dried, mid-drip, down the edges. Taki put his lips around the tip and sucked till the cookie turned pasty-soft in his mouth.

"How are you, Dad?" Mary asked. She hugged her father, feeling his bones beneath the sagging muscle of his back.

"How am I?" he sighed. "I'm glad you're here, Mary—you and the kids."

"And Mom? How is she?"

Papou peered over his shoulder at the kids. Loukia's pinky was extended as she nibbled on her cookie. "Your mother found butter from God-knows-where. She baked exactly five cookies— five in the whole batch! She wanted them to be done right. No skimping."

"So she's well?"

"So she's...she's excited about seeing the kids."

Taki drew the sweet liquid down his throat.

"And Philip?" Mary asked.

"I don't know where Philip is right now," Papou Yiorgos said. He looked around the verandah, evading Mary's gaze. "But I *do* know where Yiayia Evantheia is: she's on the *platia*, and she's very anxious to see her beautiful grandchildren." He clapped his hands together. "What do you say, kids? Should we go to the *platia* to find your *yiayia*?"

The kids jumped and giggled, grabbing their grandfather's hand. They all seemed younger when they were together, Mary thought. She watched the threesome skip down the road, toward the *platia*, singing a made-up song.

"I'll join you later," she called, as if any of them were listening.

Mary breathed in, establishing herself here, in Zagora, on her parents' verandah. The wildflowers were encroaching onto the stone, she noticed. And the grapevines—they needed pruning. She placed her hand on the spiky bark.

"They won't trust me with the shears." The voice was slurred, the mouth lugubrious.

Mary whipped her head around. Her brother stood, lopsided, in the doorway of the house.

"Hello, Philip," she said politely. "It's good to see you." She approached her brother with measured steps. She kissed him twice, once on each cheek. The greeting reminded Philip of the way his sister had welcomed some of the officers' wives at Easter—graceful and distanced, as if keeping her makeup and outfit untouched.

"Hello, Mary," Philip said. "Mary, Mary, Mary." He lifted his top lip to reveal his teeth. His mouth opened, slow and controlled, till his jaw was fully extended. Then Philip cackled.

"Philip!"

"Mary."

Philip's lips clamped into an intense seriousness. "I am very pleased to see you, Mary." He cackled again, and limped inside.

Taki scheduled his days around one paramount imperative: to avoid his uncle. He spent most afternoons at the beach, since Philip didn't seem able to hike down the mountain. At night, he slept in the parlour; his other option was to share a bed with Philip.

Taki was still asleep in the parlour when a man grunted past him, carrying a large burlap sack on his shoulder. His opposite arm wavered in the air, balancing him. His neck was contorted to the side.

"Just take them upstairs," Yiayia Evantheia said, pointing up the dim staircase. "Dump them on the floor, in that first room."

The farmer gave a truncated nod, restricted as he was by the sack. He, along with several other men, was hauling the year's almond harvest. Their women—wives, daughters, nieces, cousins, surreptitious lovers—they would soon come to the Samsarelos house to shuck the nuts, for which they'd be paid piecemeal, a fraction of a cent per almond.

"Get up, Taki," Mary said brusquely. She wanted to leave the house before the cabal of village women arrived. She began packing a bag for the beach. "We'll be leaving soon. As soon as we can."

"Where are you going?" Philip's hand landed on his sister's shoulder, close to the neck. She spun around to see his face smiling down.

"To the beach," she twittered, trying to seem nonplussed.

"I think I'll go with you," he said grandly, sticking out his chest.

"Oh...but, Philip...do you think you can? The path is very, very steep...."

Philip's eyelids peeled back.

"But, of course, if you think you can." Mary spoke quickly. She took one step backward, increasing the distance between them. "You know the path. It was silly of me to suggest..."

Philip's lips shot into a smile. His eyes remained staring. "Mary, Mary, Mary, Mary, Mary, Mary, Mary": he breathed out her name. As he breathed in, the name became a sucking sound in his throat: "Mary, Mary, Mary, Mary, Mary, Mary, Mary."

"I'll just get the towels, and..."

Mary left Taki alone with his uncle, who swayed and

hummed, his eyes closed. For the first time since the war, Taki let himself examine his uncle's face. The crater was deep above Philip's right eye, where the bone plunged inward. The skin had become corrugated with bands of scarring, each one unnaturally white and smooth. His cheekbones, once pronounced, were buried beneath fat and swollen flesh.

"Hell-oooo."

Taki's muscles jumped. His uncle's eyes had opened; he'd been watching Taki.

"Hi, Uncle Philip," Taki said.

"Are you ready to swim today?" Philip's arms radiated through the air. "You gonna swim with me?"

Taki blinked as his uncle's hands cut close to his face. "I think I'll...try to...to help with...the nuts. Here."

"No!" Philip's hands smacked onto his head. "No, Taki!" He pulled on his hair, then hobbled onto the verandah. "Have a good day!"

Taki scurried up the stairs. "Excuse me," he said to a farmer who was returning to the verandah to retrieve another sack.

Taki took refuge on a stool in Philip's room. The furniture had been pushed against the walls, making space for the almonds and women. Taki's legs bobbled. He watched the farmers slit the burlap sacks with razors. Once the sack was cut, they'd dump the green almonds onto the floor, sending them clacking toward the corner where the house was angled down. After an hour, the almonds had buried Taki's feet, encircling his ankles.

By now, the women had begun to arrive. They waded through the almonds, carrying their stools into a circle on the floor. Taki recognized the women, though he knew the name of only one: Sophia, their neighbour with the large forehead and a gnarled dark mole on her cheek.

"Hello, Taki," she said, rustling his hair. "Will you join us? It'll be fun!" Her smile was a tiny half-circle in the middle of her thick-jawed face.

"I don't know what to do," Taki said.

"Just watch," Sophia replied. "You'll learn by watching."

Several women now sat on stools, their knees apart, their skirts stretched, forming aprons between their legs. They would scoop the nuts onto their laps, and work from that pile. The task was more manageable that way, Sophia told Taki. "Otherwise, you'd never feel like you were getting anywhere," she said, gesturing to the floor, one foot deep in balls of almonds.

Taki observed Sophia's technique and attempted to mimic her. She leaned forward, elbows on knees, back rounded. With her thumbnail, she pierced into the seam of the nut's casing. The moist outer covering could be peeled back without any tools, as long as the action of the fingers was firm and unrushed, otherwise the casing would tear. Taki often failed to remove the casing intact; he'd be forced, then, to pick at the skin, removing one small section at a time.

The women discarded the empty casings onto the floor. The hard nuts underneath were oval and striated. These were tossed into metal buckets. Yiayia Evantheia would count them at the end of the day, and determine each woman's payment.

"You're very fast," Sophia said to a young black-haired woman.

"I have long nails—it makes it easier." She ran her nail back and forth over the seam. "Stavros likes them long," she added, tossing back her hair.

"Hey," another woman said. "Be careful with Stavros. I hear Stavroula has long nails, too."

The black-haired woman thrust her thumbnail down. "Who told you that?"

"The moon was very, very bright last Sunday. It tells you a lot, our moon."

"Really..." The black-haired woman slid a finger underneath the casing and circled the nut inside. "When, exactly, was the moon bright? After the wedding?"

"Yes, *koukla*. The moon spoke loud and clear after the wedding. In the meadow behind the church. No question."

Sophia nudged Taki. "What do you think of all this talk?"

Taki's shoulders crept up, sheepish. "It's really fun," he said, thrilled to admit to this vaguely illicit pleasure.

Sophia giggled at the boy, then kissed his head with her small puckered lips.

"Um," Sophia said, "speaking of weddings...do you think Philip's ever going to get married?"

"Who would marry him now?" the black-haired woman said.

Sophia gathered some nuts in her hands. A few overflowed, tumbling down. "I would," she said.

"Oh, Sophia... Philip has changed."

"I know," she replied. "I don't care."

"Listen, Sophia," the black-haired woman continued. "We are in this bedroom with our legs spread and some Samsarelos nuts in our lap. The *only* reason we're here is because we're getting paid. That's the *only* reason we're in this room."

"He needs someone to take care of him."

"You'll be his maid," a woman said.

"I'll be his wife."

The landscape of the floor had changed. The green balls had been replaced by hollow casings, which lay gaping and broken.

"I love him," Sophia said.

"You love what he was."

"Yes," Sophia said. "I do. And that hasn't gone away. He's still Philip. It's not like his whole—his—everything he was before...it's not like that just disappears. People don't just lose their whole past like that."

The black-haired woman reached across Taki to squeeze Sophia's hand. Her skin was scratched in tight lines, evidence of the hours she'd toiled, picking almonds and apples from the Samsareloses' trees. "But their past can get taken, Sophia."

Sophia brought the woman's hand to her lips, giving a quick kiss to each of her fingers. "I don't believe that," she said.

Taki's nine-day stretch of avoiding Philip ended that night. Both uncle and nephew were forced to sleep in the parlour, since Philip's bedroom was awash in almonds.

"Tell me something," Philip said. He lay face-down on the couch. Taki was nearby, lying on a sheet placed over the worn carpet. He could feel the knobs of his spine digging into the floor. "Tell—me—some—thing."

Taki didn't say anything; he thought he might pretend he'd fallen asleep.

Philip swatted the side of Taki's head. "You're awake, Taki, so just tell me."

"Tell you what, Uncle Philip?"

"Tell me why my parents keep that trophy." He pointed to the bronze object displayed in the centre of the piano, atop a hand-carved wood pedestal.

Taki had first seen that trophy several years earlier, at his home in Thessaloniki. "I don't know why," Taki said.

"Guess."

"Uncle Philip, I don't—"

"Taki!" Philip shoved his face over the edge of the couch. His black bangs hung down, brushing against Taki's forehead. "Taki, Taki: you're not dumb, Taki. Think: why would they keep it." He smiled with serene satisfaction.

"I don't—"

Philip bit the air. "Think!" he said through bared teeth.

Taki turned his eyes aside, afraid to move his head. "Because," Taki whimpered. "Because you won it, and they're proud of you."

Philip sighed and lay back on the couch. "Very close," he said. "It's because I won it, and they *were* proud of me. They *were.* Past tense. Past. The trophy reminds them." Philip propped himself on his elbows, his neck hyper-extended, his face upside-down. "Do you realize my mother cradles that thing at night? She comes here and pets the trophy."

Taki curled onto his side.

"Did you realize my mother hasn't touched me since I left the hospital? Nothing. Not a hug. Not a handshake. Not a fucking slap on the face. Nothing."

Cringing, Taki waited to hear a cackle or cry: nothing.

"Hey, Taki, don't get upset. You don't need to be afraid of me." Philip flipped onto his belly. He stroked Taki's shoulder.

"I'm not, Uncle Philip."

The stroke became a punch, just one—not too hard, but hard enough. "You don't need to lie, Taki," Philip said soothingly. "Please, don't ever lie. Please." Philip scratched his forehead. "Ask me a question."

"I don't know what to ask."

"Anything. Ask me when I took a piss, or what I ate for dinner, or how many men I killed in Epirus.... Ask me anything." Philip shook Taki's shoulder. "Don't cry," he said. "Really. It's okay. Ask me."

"I don't—"

"Ask anyway. Ask anything. Ask, ask, ask." He pumped Taki's shoulder. "Ask, ask, ask."

"Does it hurt," Taki said, the words shaky. "Your forehead and your ankle—do they hurt?"

"No. Now ask something else."

"Did it hurt when it happened?"

"Ankle yes, forehead no. Next."

"Umm... I don't—"

"You know what to ask, Taki: ask. What do you want to know. Ask, ask, ask, ask—"

"Were you scared?"

"Ankle yes, forehead no. Next."

"Umm..."

"Next."

"I don't—"

"Next."

"Uncle—"

"Next, next, next, next: ankle forehead, ankle forehead, ankle forehead: next, next, next, next—"

"Why are they different!" Taki cried it out; he didn't want to hear his uncle's voice anymore—not his questions, not his answers.

"Because they didn't happen at the same time," Philip said. "Next question—just ask it. Ankle forehead, ankle forehead."

"They didn't happen—"

"Nope. Ankle on the battlefield; forehead on the pavement. Battlefield pavement, battlefield pavement: ask."

"Pavement? I don't—"

"Good, Taki. You're very good, you know. You're smart, like your mother. And your uncle." He snorted. "You're smart, my little Taki." Philip released Taki's shoulder. "Ask your question. Pavement: what's strange about pavement?"

"I don't—"

"I'll tell you a secret." Philip hung his torso over the couch again. "The pavement?" he said, nodding. "The pavement? The pavement, Taki, was outside the hospital, underneath the window. And the *real* secret..." His eyes changed shape as he spoke, rounding from oval to disc. "The *real* secret is that I have never been so free, Taki, as when my face broke apart. Do you understand, Taki?"

"I don't know, Uncle Philip."

Philip pulled himself back onto the couch. "You're too young to understand, Taki. Thank you for being truthful about that. No one else is truthful about anything." Philip's voice got loud, though it didn't frighten Taki anymore: it was theatrical now, not bellicose. "I am the great war hero, shot in the ankle and the forehead. I am the tragic soldier gunned down to protect his country." Philip chuckled. "That's what they say I am. That's the story everyone is told. I'll play along, if they want me to. So long as I get to *play* along—play it up, fuck it up, fuck with all of them."

Taki tucked his legs to his chest. He could smell the new green of the almond casings on his skin.

"Uncle Philip?"

"Yes, Taki."

"Are you playing with me right now, Uncle Philip?"

Philip rubbed his cratered forehead. "I don't know, Taki," he said. "Honestly...I honestly don't know."

Mary decided to return to the city the following day, two weeks ahead of schedule. She said she wanted to be closer to Agamemnon during the occupation. Philip said a solemn goodbye to Mary and Loukia. He then winked at Taki, or perhaps he merely blinked. Taki couldn't quite tell—not with the lopsidedness of his uncle's face.

Twenty-Six
Autumn 1942

The German soldier arrived one afternoon in late fall. Loukia was the only person awake in the house when he rapped on the wooden door. Private Benedikt had determined that this type of knock—brisk—established his authority best; the doorbell didn't have the same effect.

Loukia was transcribing her notes from school when she heard the knock. This was her usual studying strategy: rewrite all the data, neater and in bullet form. In this way, she'd gain mastery of the material.

The Peloponnesian Wars:
A) The first History ever written.
B) Method: Thucydides gathered stories BUT he didn't trust any of them. He wanted facts not myths. What are facts?
C) Historian chooses what to include/exclude. Makes <u>interre-</u>
<u>lationships</u> *bet. events. Without interrelationships, facts mean nothing. Historian's task: make lines between events &*

Loukia assumed a villager was at the door, seeking Agamemnon's help with his horse or cow. She skipped down the hallway, hoping it was Laspiti.

"*Yia sou. Eimai Benedikt.*" The soldier extended his hand toward Loukia, crossing the threshold of the house. Loukia's arms remained at her sides. Benedikt smiled wearily. During his rounds of the neighbourhood, not one Greek had ever taken his hand—some out of fear, others out of pride. He couldn't tell which controlled this girl. "May I come in, please." He brought his hand back, instinctively touching the brass buttons on his jacket. Loukia said nothing.

The soldier wore shiny black boots over the mass of his calves. His pants ballooned out at the thigh, beneath a leather belt. Around his arm was a band of cloth, constricting his biceps, the swastika black in a field of white. Benedikt removed his hat. He crouched on one knee so Loukia was taller than him. "Are your parents home?"

"No," she said.

"Your grandparents?"

"They're sleeping."

"May I look around. That's all I need to do—just look." His grammar was correct, his vocabulary precise. Even so, Loukia's language seemed strange coming from this man's mouth; he made the words resonate in different parts of him.

"May I...?"

Loukia didn't invite Private Benedikt inside, nor did she resist when he stepped past her. She pressed herself against the doors to the dining room and listened as this big German man—this uniformed, armed, big Nazi man—wandered through her house. She heard his footsteps in the kitchen, which made the glasses clang against each other. His boots then tromped up the stairs and traversed the hallway. She heard them pause; she grabbed the fabric of her skirt and waited for those boots to begin again. She feared that sound—the unquestioned entitlement of those steps in the hallway, on the rug, beside the bedroom where Taki slept, alone. Loukia folded her arms over her chest now; her shirt was damp with sweat, though she was shivering. The boots thudded above her. They moved assuredly down the stairs.

The soldier smiled at Loukia. He didn't want to scare her. He was only looking, like he said; he was only trying to locate houses that could accommodate German officers, that's all. That's all he was doing. He was just a German teenager who had studied Greek, and was therefore chosen for this simple job. He was also told to determine, while he was searching through these houses, whether any Jews were hiding inside.

"Three bedrooms," Benedikt said. "That's good." He stood before Loukia. His skin seemed scraped raw; Loukia had seen rashes like that on the older boys in school—those who'd shaved before they'd grown enough hair. "And what's in here?" he asked, stepping toward her.

Instinctively, Loukia spread her arms to the sides, as if protecting something precious. Benedikt stopped. His gaze intensified, seeking knowledge from her expression.

"What's in there, little girl?"

"Nothing. It's just..."

"Is there someone in there?" He reached for the handle, pushing her aside without force. "I need to check whether someone's in there."

"No, there's no one," Loukia said. "It's just... The room is..."

Benedikt walked through the double doors.

"The room is special, that's all...."

The dining room changed with Benedikt inside it. The mysterious sophistication became childish; the fairy-tale frescoes—those fat cherubs with their bare bottoms and blond ringlet curls—they seemed garish now, with Benedikt's eyes on them. It's special, Loukia insisted, silently.

Benedikt checked all the corners, underneath the piano and behind the curtains. There were no crumbs on the floors, no stray pencils. Benedikt was quickly satisfied that no one was hiding here, in this pretty room. "Okay," he told Loukia. "I've seen what I need to see." Benedikt rested his hand on the piano's lowermost keys as he spoke. He longed to press them down, to make a sound, a chord. A piece was laid open on the stand: a waltz. He looked at the score's changing contours, the black notes getting more dense on the page, reaching up then dissolving down, into the lone beat of a pause. He had played this piece before. His muscles remembered its music.

"Tell your parents I'll be back tomorrow," he said, sliding past Loukia.

"Should I get the door?" Taki asked. He was embarrassed for his grandmother. She'd sat on the couch all day, a towel wrapped around her head. She wore a bathrobe over her clothes.

"No!" Yiayia Loukia said. "I'll handle this! I said I'd handle it, and I will handle it...." Taki watched his grandmother shuffle and mumble her way to the door.

Yiayia Loukia had heard about the Nazi's visit, his intention to make the house "a hotel for a Hun," as she put it. She declared that she would take care of it. No one believed that she would.

"Hello, good day," Benedikt said. He stood beside a tall man whose chest was shiny with medals. This man, Benedikt's superior, was not pleased at the moment. The Jewish ghetto was becoming difficult to patrol; the Greek guerrillas—"ELAS," they called themselves—had killed four soldiers in the city; and, most disturbingly, a viaduct had been bombed further south. This act of sabotage—intricate, effective, with consequences as yet untold—was clear evidence that British Special Operatives were here in the country, collaborating with ELAS. "Tell her we're looking for homes—"

"Oooo," Yiayia Loukia moaned. "Oooo!" She held her forehead, then grasped at her throat. "Good day, day good...ooooo!" She opened and closed her mouth several times, not making a sound.

Benedikt paled. The officer addressed Benedikt, who responded rapidly, his head shaking. "*Nein, nein,*" he kept saying.

Yiayia Loukia began coughing, without covering her mouth. "Ooooo..." She hacked and hit her chest, bringing up phlegm that she spit in her palm.

The officer's face curdled.

Yiayia Loukia stared at her hand in fascination. She spread her fingers so the phlegm made a webbing. "Ooooo!"

"Thank you," Benedikt said. "That's all we require for now."

Yiayia Loukia watched the officers go. "Ooooo!" she moaned one last time, then shut the door. "There," she said. "Let them find somewhere else to stay." She took off her robe and went to the kitchen to wash her hands.

"That was very good, Yiayia!" Taki said.

"Yes, it was. I know what I'm ing-do. Know I." Yiayia Loukia still wore the towel on her head. She touched her hand to it, as if fluffing a fine coiffure.

Twenty-Seven
Winter 1942

Levon was sweeping glass off the sidewalk when the family returned from church. Mary had invited Costa and Katarina for tea. All the adults, Loukia included, strolled through the gate without talking to the grocer. "That's it—keep the sidewalk clean!" Yiayia Loukia scowled. "He should do that time the all. He's just lazy, that Armenian."

A handkerchief fell from Levon's pocket. Its whiteness was patterned with blurred red circles.

"All Armenians are lazy! All of them."

Taki headed toward Levon. "I think you dropped this," he said, handing him the cloth.

"Thank you, Taki," he said.

Taki looked aside and down, trying—without success—not to stare at Levon's face. The left eye was swollen and shiny from a yellowish discharge. Underneath the glint, the flesh had turned purple-black.

Levon adjusted his glasses. He flinched as the rim hit his skin. "It's ugly, isn't it."

"I didn't mean to—"

"It's okay. It's natural to look." Levon removed his glasses, wiping the encrusted fluid off the top of his left lens. "I was roasting the chickpeas in the back," he explained. "The Nazi patrol saw the light. I didn't think... You know, I was in the back, and I thought for sure it was dark up front.... Careless."

Taki nodded. "Are you okay, Levon?" he asked.

Levon smiled at the boy. Several churchgoers stepped onto

the street, avoiding Levon and the glass. No one had, until now, inquired about Levon's well-being. "Hey, Taki, would you like to help me out? I have a job for you."

Taki thought about the tea time inside the house, with Yiayia Loukia and Papou Efstratios lodged on the couch, and the men talking in low tones, and the women's mysterious laughter. "Okay," Taki said.

"Come on inside."

Taki followed Levon into the store. The front window was completely gone. The industrial metal grinder had been knocked over, leaving a gash in the wood floor.

"I don't know how I'll haul that thing up...." Levon put one hand on the funnel, the other on the teeth of the grinder's wheels. He pushed. His exertion didn't seem to act on the object at all. It sat. "Two kids got it down, and I'll need a horse to lift it." Levon stood up, too quick, an exclamation of pain issuing from his mouth.

"Are you—"

"Yes. It's nothing." Levon bit on his lower lip. "So," he continued, "do you think you can sort out the beans, Taki?"

"Um...I think so."

The floor was a carpet of herbs, spices, grains, beans. The wood boards of the shelves were largely cleared, their contents spilled on the ground. The scale was broken beside the register: one of six metal chains had been ripped from the crossbar. The instrument was crumpled toward the right, one plate suspended in the air, the other heavy on the countertop. Hanging from the pipes on the ceiling were three burlap sacks, none of them completely empty. The weight of them swayed as Levon walked past.

"Okay," Levon said, bringing a sieve from the back of the store. "This'll help."

Taki retrieved a metal scoop from the floor. He dug into the debris, then dumped his catch into the sieve, which he shook from side to side. The small bits disappeared; they flowed so fast, Taki couldn't even see them fall. The dry, hard beans were all that remained, bouncing about.

"What's this one?" he asked, pointing to an unfamiliar brown bean.

Levon rubbed it with his thumb. "If you wipe off the cinnamon, Takouli, you'll see that it's actually white underneath. It's a lima." He dropped it in a glass bin. "Put the limas here, chickpeas in this one, almonds here. And...whatever else goes here. Okay?"

"Okay, Levon." Taki kept scooping and shaking. His little fingers worked fast.

"They were just kids," Levon said. He was untying one of the burlap sacks. "Stupid kids... German soldiers, yes—but they're just teenagers! They didn't even take the coffee, and that's worth a fortune right now." The cut on Levon's cheek was covered by a globule of blood.

"What did they take, Levon?" Taki looked up at the man. "Did they take your money?"

Levon shook his head and lowered his arms. He focused his gaze on the boy. Taki's hair was getting long, the waves threatening to become curls. His whole face was soft—round nose, full lips, smooth cheeks. He must be ten or eleven now, Levon thought. Levon's daughter had been eleven when she was killed in Armenia. Her hair had been curly—really tightly curly, unruly and free. "What did they take..." Levon muttered. He wiped his cheek, smearing the blood. "Nothing you can carry," he said. Levon rubbed his thumb against his fingers, mixing the blood with the dust.

Taki watched the flakes drift, red, to the ground.

Taki was glad to get back to school the following morning. The pressures here were all-encompassing: writing exams, reading aloud, waiting for Gondicas's scorn. These stresses were real for

Taki; they gave him relief from the rest.

"The exam will be tomorrow—three hours, exactly—covering all the mythological figures we've discussed since the beginning of the year."

Aliki raised her hand, her arm pressed against her ear.

"There will be multiple-choice questions, plus two essays."

Nikos slid forward in his seat, then pushed himself back. His shoulders squirmed.

"Do you have a problem, Nikos? You seem pained." Gondicas adjusted his vest over his girth. He was the only person who'd gotten fatter during the war.

"No, sir," Nikos said.

"Good." Gondicas turned toward the board. Nikos stuck out his chest and pulled in his chin, embodying the gluttony of authority. Dimitra tried not to giggle.

"Principal Gondicas?" Aliki's hand became jittery. She waved it about to get his attention, though he wasn't facing her. "Principal Gondicas?"

"Yes," he sighed.

"All the mythological figures? From the plays *and* the poems? Or—"

"Just what I said, Aliki."

She panicked to remember what he had said.

"Now. To Book Twelve. Nikos, we'll start with you."

"I made straight for the ship, roused up the men
to get aboard and cast off at the stern."

Nikos recited rowdily. Gondicas crossed his arms and paced before the class.

"But soon an off-shore breeze blew to our liking—
a canvas-bellying breeze, a lusty shipmate

sent by the singing nymph with sunbright hair.
So we made fast the braces, and we rested,
letting the wind and steersman work the ship.
The crew being now silent before me, I
addressed them, sore at heart."

"Now Taki."

                    "Dear friends,
more than one man, or two, should know those things
Kirke foresaw for us and shared with me,
so let me tell her forecast: then we die
with our eyes open, if we are going to die,
or know what death we baffle if we can."

Taki faltered. "Keep going," Gondicas said.

                    "Sirens
weaving a haunting song over the sea
we are to shun, she said, and their green shore
all sweet with clover; yet she urged that I
alone should listen to their song. Therefore
you are to tie me up, tight as a splint,
erect along the mast, lashed to the mast,
and if I shout and beg to be untied,
take more turns of rope to muffle me."

"That was fine, Taki. Thank you. Loukia, you next."
Taki sighed and sat back, relieved to be done.

"I rather dwelt on this part of the forecast,
while our good ship made time, bound outward down
the wind for the strange island of Sirens.

Then all at once the wind fell, and a calm
came over all the sea, as though some power
lulled the swell."

Nikos liked having Loukia in class. She was... He couldn't say, exactly. She was different—mature, maybe. Nikos looked over at the girl. Her hand circled, as if evoking the words. The fabric between her shirt-buttons parted as she took a breath and recited:

"They tied me up, then, plumb
amidships, back to the mast, lashed to the mast,
and took themselves again to rowing."

Yes, Nikos thought, that was it: she was...mature.
Dimitra was next. She spoke the song of the Sirens.

"Sweet coupled airs we sing.
No lonely seafarer
Holds clear of entering
Our green mirror.

Pleased by each purling note
Like honey twining
From her throat and my throat
Who lies—"

The air-raid siren blasted into the room, overtaking Dimitra's voice.

"Orderly!" Gondicas bellowed, though the children couldn't hear. "Orderly to the shelter!"

The students ran down the stairs, into the sun, ducking as if the ground was safe, was home.

"Orderly!"

Taki raced into the shelter behind Dimitra. There was a stumble, a slam, a bracing to stop collapse and crush. There were engines, the fire of anti-aircraft—guns suspended between the former homes of Jews—the homes of former Jews—the four-chambered guns beating out their fire: *ack-ack-ack-ack*: reverberating off the homes, into the air, the shelter, Taki's skin: *ack-ack-ack-ack*: Taki's body, vibrating.

There was fear.

"It's done."

The noise stopped long before they heard the quiet.

Long before, though time made no sense inside that space.

The students left the shelter, orderly.

"The exam begins at 9 a.m. tomorrow," Gondicas said. "Nine a.m. All the figures in myth." Gondicas's right hand trembled, palsied. He grasped it in his left. "Everyone go home now. Go home and study."

Gondicas's mother hooked her arm through her son's. "Go home, children," she said. "Be with your mothers now." Gondicas's mother led her son toward her house.

The students milled about, unwilling to venture far.

"That one wasn't very long," Nikos said, lifting a tuft of grass with his toes.

"Nah. It was easy."

"Yeah."

"It was short."

"Yup."

"Dimitra!" Loukia gasped. "There's blood on your cheek!"

Dimitra wiped her face and looked at her fingers, not believing. "I don't think I'm cut.... I—"

"It's from me," Taki whispered, holding up his hand. "I think it's from me."

"What?" Dimitra turned to him, concerned.

"I scraped my hand on the concrete. It's nothing." Taki covered his wound.

"It's from...?" his sister asked.

"I tripped—"

"But only because *I* tripped," Dimitra said.

"Right. And I didn't want to fall on you, so I...and then I must've...my hand must've..." Until that moment, Taki hadn't been aware that he'd held Dimitra through the bombing; he would never fully realize that she had held him, too.

"Do you need a bandage, Taki? Are you—"

"Excuse me," a man said. His face was becalmed. Taki recognized him as Gondicas's other next-door neighbour. "But there's an anti-aircraft shell in our house."

"In your *house*?" Nikos said.

"It fell through the roof." He positioned his hands two feet apart, indicating the size of the object.

"Are you okay?"

"It didn't explode. It's just...sitting there." He spoke in a level voice. He nodded his head, then started walking away.

Loukia glanced at Nikos. "We have to *do* something!" she said. "We can't just let him leave! He's scared, he's—"

"Let's get Gondicas," Nikos replied boldly, gazing at Loukia. She had the most erotic space between her front teeth when she smiled, which she was doing, now, at him. Nikos's muscles, blood-filled from the raid, now moved fast. He grabbed Loukia's hand with purpose; they hurried to Gondicas's parlour.

"Should we look?" Dimitra asked, mischief in her smile.

"Look at what?"

"At the shell. He said it's in the house...."

Taki probed around the pulpy wound on his hand. "I'll go if you go," he answered. The girl had already gone. She was easing through the bushes, heading directly for the shattered window.

"My God..." she said. The ceiling was ruptured. Wood beams hung down around the edges of the hole. Directly below was the dining room table, demolished. In the spot where a pitcher once stood lay a long metal object, seemingly inert.

"I dare you to go inside," Dimitra said.

"No way," Taki answered. "It could explode!"

"It won't explode. Watch: I'll prove it." Dimitra was taking off her jacket. She swiped the windowsill with the bunched-up garment, knocking off the broken glass.

"Careful!" Taki said.

She arced one leg over the sill. Now straddling the stone, she lowered her body inside the house. Her grey skirt rose, revealing her thighs and the white elastic higher up. She hopped fully inside, pulling her skirt down after.

"My God..." Taki echoed.

Dimitra crept around the table on tiptoe, staring at the shell in the centre. *Bullet*—that was the word that came to Taki's mind. The shell was a bullet of the Giants, if the Giants had bullets, which they didn't, Taki thought, watching the girl, waiting for her to come outside, to him, safe from the bullet that might explode, suddenly, ripping her.

Dimitra squared her shoulders to face Taki. She waved and smiled, thrilled with herself and this craziness.

"Careful..." Taki whispered. He'd heard that word enough to know it meant nothing. "Careful..."

Dimitra bent down, disrupting the dust in the air. She picked some wood off the floor. Then she tiptoed back to the window, lifting herself up and through.

"The shell is huge!" she said.

"I can't believe you did that."

"And look—I found a piece of shrapnel, too." She showed Taki the hunk of wood, blackened on one side. "Feel it—it's still hot," she said. Taki ran his hand along the length of the wood, smooth and warm, the skin of something alive. His hand cupped the bottom, which was a spray of splinters. Taki rotated his wrist, feeling the pricks in his palm.

"You can keep it," Dimitra said. "It's a present. To remember today." She smiled at Taki, no longer so mischievous. "Now," she said, "I'd better study for the exam."

"Nine a.m.," Taki joked, assuming Gondicas's voice.

"Exactly three hours."

"All the figures."

The kids laughed.

Taki was studying in bed that night when he heard the gunshot. He froze in place, his belly sickly warm; he listened while his father rushed to investigate, returning to report that he needed to notify the authorities immediately. He hoped, he said to Mary, "the dogs didn't get at it first." Taki turned off the lantern and tried to sleep. Cerberus was the dog of the Underworld, the hound of Hades. Someone got past him...someone....

Taki got out of bed early the next morning. He wasn't sure whether the sun was up; light couldn't penetrate the blackout drapes. The exam began at 9 a.m., exactly.

Galatea was turned from marble into flesh, Taki recited in his mind. And Adonis's flesh was ripped apart by wild dogs.... Taki gathered his notes from the floor beside his bed and went downstairs.

His father's papers were organized in neat piles on the parlour table.

Contact with Cairo Gov't: Update from Maki
Distribution of Pamphlets: Update from Agamemnon
and Costa

Taki felt dark excitement as he read: this was secret information. His father was a spy, or a special operative, or... Whatever he was, it was important.

Tracking down ELAS Camp—# of men and weapons,
planned attacks, etc. Update from Yianni

Agamemnon's handwriting was angular and compressed.
Taki wasn't sure he'd read that line right: *# of men and weapons,*
planned attacks, etc.

Papou Efstratios groaned in his sleep. Taki went outside,
the excitement now acidic in his empty belly. He stood in his
pyjamas and looked at the bare fig tree. Taki tried to recall which
god turned Actaeon into a tree. It was Artemis, he thought. Or
Aphrodite. He sighed.

"Over here," a man's voice said.

Taki turned toward the laneway between his house and the
apartment building.

"Uh!" a second man grunted. They were garbagemen, wearing their dirty uniforms. "What a mess!"

Taki was standing on tiptoe, leaning over the backyard railing.

"How the hell are we gonna do this." The second garbageman put his fists on his hips and stared down at the ground,
which Taki couldn't quite see.

"I'll take the feet, you take the armpits," the first garbageman said.

"*You* take the armpits! This is disgusting!"

"Just take the armpits, okay! There'll be more—you can
choose next time."

"Great. What a choice."

The men crouched down; they were grappling with something. Taki knew it was a body—*armpits, feet, a mess*—but the
body was a "something": an object, not a person. It was an "it"
that the dogs would get at. It wasn't a "he," Taki told himself.

Not Spiros.

Spiros, who'd survived Epirus, who'd been smoking a cigarette, which was spotted by a German soldier, who was patrolling

for violations of the blackout order, which included the cigarette's orange glow, which became the soldier's target, which he hit, with precision.

"What a way to go," the first garbageman said. "Poor bastard."

"Yeah, well...just hurry up," the second said. "This poor bastard's brains are dripping on my shoes."

The exam starts at 9 a.m. exactly, Taki thought. Exactly 9 a.m. Theseus killed the Minotaur and Perseus slew Medusa and Actaeon was turned into a tree. Nine a.m. Taki bent forward. He hoped to vomit but dry-heaved instead: his stomach was empty.

The test began. Nine a.m.

Twenty-Eight
Spring 1943

Mary opened the kitchen window wide, though the air was chilly on her wet hands. She'd hauled a table and chairs onto the back porch for her in-laws. She'd given them the newspaper, the knitting needles, cups of tea and extra cigarettes. They would remain outside, she resolved; after a wintertime of those two stationed in the parlour, Mary needed a little privacy, even if she was only cleaning the kitchen. She hummed as she scrubbed chickpea scum off the inside of a pot. She hoped she hadn't given her in-laws too much tea: she didn't want them coming inside to use the toilet every ten minutes. Mary rinsed the pot, her wedding ring clinking on the ceramic as she turned it under the stream of water. Her humming turned to singing, and no one was there to command her to stop. Mary was in the middle of a raucous war song when the doorbell rang.

Eleni Bouloucas stood at the top of the staircase, looking down at the city bustling beneath her. The farmer who'd given her a ride from the village was turning his cart onto a side street, toward the market. She came on a day when her nephew, Dimitri Laspiti, would be in the fields. He'd told her, specifically, that she shouldn't get involved; he'd said she didn't understand the implications of the information she possessed.

A trolley glided past. Dozens of faces, ghostly, looked out the windows; dozens of people pressed into each other, and none of them spoke. Eleni shook her head, clucking her tongue. The cities severed all connections between people. There was nothing here to bind them together, one person to the next. Not like in the villages.

Eleni could hear footsteps inside, coming down the hall. She was sure, from their rhythm, that no one had brought the news to this house. People walked and smelled differently in those first hours of a crisis: Eleni had witnessed enough such moments to know.

The woman smiled piteously when Mary opened the door. "Mrs. Apostolides?" she said. "I'm a friend, from the villages. May I come in?"

Mary's chest expanded in a deeply annoyed sigh. "Of course," she said. She forced a polite smile that didn't quite materialize. "I'll put on water for tea."

Eleni perched herself on the parlour couch. She examined the handmade blanket. The pattern was flawed in one square, toward the edge, where the diamond was one stitch too large. That was unacceptable, really. She dropped the blanket and folded her hands in her lap. The room was clean, at least.

"I take milk in my tea," she called. "Not honey, just milk."

The pot lid trembled, on cue. "I'll give you whatever milk we have, Mrs.... What's your name? I don't even know."

"Mrs. Bouloucas. I'm Constantia Laspiti's aunt." Eleni Bouloucas had never married. Her older sister—Constantia's mother—had taken the family's dowry money. Eleni was now well past menopause. She'd never been with a man. But she knew all about men, and women, too, and their treachery toward each other.

Eleni stared at the day-old newspaper on the table, though she couldn't read. Her greasy hair fell around her face. Mary could see flecks of dirt or scabs on her scalp, along the crooked line where her hair was parted. "So," Mary said, "you wanted to talk?" Mary poured the tea. She didn't serve any food.

"Yes...but...I don't know how to say it." Eleni always started with that line; it was usually effective. "I just don't know..."

Mary held her cup to her lips but didn't drink. Eleni noticed the warm gold of Mary's wedding band, the manicured fingernails uniformly long and curved. She met Mary's gaze. "Mrs. Apostolides," she said. "Something's happening in the villages. The communists...they are getting organized. They're... doing things."

"What things?" Mary lowered her cup.

"The specifics aren't important," Eleni said. She monitored Mary for a response—a bend in the spine, or a rapidity of blinking.

Mary put the saucer on the table with excessive delicacy. "So what *is* important?"

Eleni straightened her back, then lowered her chin, extending the moment. "Listen to me, Mrs. Apostolides. Don't let Agamemnon come to the villages." She liked using Agamemnon's first name; Mrs. Apostolides wasn't expecting this. "Agamemnon is not safe. They know him. You must not let him come to the villages anymore."

Mary's eyelids fluttered. "I don't understand."

"There's nothing to understand, Mrs. Apostolides. I've told you all you need to know. And now..." Eleni said, rising from the couch. "Now I must go."

"Stay a little!" Mary said, jumping up. "I don't understand.... Please...let's talk a bit more!"

Eleni was walking toward the door. She felt that familiar flow of serenity in her tissue: she had done her duty. She had been the purveyor of information. People responded to the truth that she provided; through her words, she changed lives, altered decisions. Sometimes these truths were painful: infidelities, financial bungles, betrayals of trust. Despite the pain, though, Eleni was certain that people deserved to know the complete reality of any given situation. This is what she offered.

Eleni put her palm gently on Mary's shoulder. "He'll be fine, Mrs. Apostolides, so long as you heed my warning." She folded her dirt-stained hands and gazed at the door. She wanted to see Mary's fine fingers open it, just for her.

"Are you ready?" Agamemnon asked.

"Yes, Dad. I can't wait to—"

"So long as you're ready. Laspiti should've been here by now."

Agamemnon stood, impatient, and thrust open a kitchen drawer. He took a knife and shaved the wood off the tip of his pencil with fast, staccato motions. The point was quite long now. He wrote on a blank sheet of paper:

Emphasize tradition and freedom.
Foreign rule: from Turks to Russia??

"We have a lot to do today," he muttered. "I wish Laspiti would arrive when he said he would. This is—"

"You're going, Agamemnon?" Mary was standing in the door between the kitchen and parlour, her arms crossed over her chest. She wore only her nightgown; her hair was loose on her shoulders.

Agamemnon inverted his lips and put the pencil down. "Yes, I'm going," he said, without looking at his wife.

"Please, Agamemnon. Please..." Mary wiped the corners of her mouth. "I don't know what she meant, but she was definitely concerned. Please don't go."

"Mary, I can't believe you've let that woman frighten you. Eleni is spooked, that's all."

"Agamemnon, please don't go," Mary said, stepping forward. "Please."

Taki had never seen his mother dressed this way. The nightgown was slightly sheer, revealing the outline of her thighs and belly, the dark circles on her breasts. Mary reached forward and clutched her husband's hands. "Please don't go." The skin over her knuckles strained white.

"Mary, stop this," Agamemnon said. "I'm going. And I'm *not* discussing this again. Last night was enough."

"Think about your children, Agamemnon. Please..."

"That's enough." Agamemnon spoke his words low in his throat, his mouth barely opening. "Stop this now."

"Agamemnon, please, please...please don't go." Mary knelt onto the floor, both knees down at once, her hands clasping his. "Please..."

"Mary." Agamemnon's voice was quivering now. "Mary, get up."

She shook her head, her hair drooping around her face. "Don't go," she sobbed.

"*Mary!*" Taki's body jumped; his hand knocked over a glass. "I said get up!" Agamemnon took a fast step back; Mary's torso fell forward onto the floor. Her mouth was within inches of Agamemnon's boot.

Taki slid off his chair and backed into the countertop. He watched his father step over his mother's body.

"Please don't go...." she said.

Agamemnon strode to the middle of the parlour, then turned abruptly. "I'll talk to you when you're behaving like an adult again. I'll talk, but I won't change my mind. I have a job to do, and I won't hide in my house."

Taki heard the back door slam shut. "Mama," he said.

"Please don't go...." she said.

"Mama?"

"Please don't go!" she shrieked.

Taki ran, out the door, into the yard, underneath the fig tree. He let his mother's cries fade into the white noise of morning, with the wheels of the garbage cart and the clomping of hooves. He played a game with a leaf and a stick, pretending they were people.

"Can we go to the beach," the leaf said to the stick man. "Can we?"

"Yes. Let's go to the beach."

"Yeah!" said the leaf in a child's voice, far younger than Taki's own. "Yeah!"

Taki heard Laspiti arrive. He heard his father call for him—once—then warn that he wouldn't call again.

The characters were silent. They tried to hold their breath.

"This is your last chance, Taki. I'm not coming back for you. Do you understand?"

The characters looked at each other but did not move. The horse started for the village.

"Can we buy a *koulouri*?" the leaf asked.

"Of course," the stick man said.

The leaf hopped in excitement. Taki played the game alone.

Laspiti's cart didn't get very far when it stopped in front of the train tracks. "Sorry I'm late," Laspiti said.

"You're very late."

"I got stuck here." He gestured to the train that passed. "They've been going all morning. From the ghetto," he added.

Agamemnon nodded. His eyes shuttled back and forth, watching the cattle cars pass, filled with their human cargo.

"So what happened? Why did Mrs. Bouloucas come to my house?"

"I'm sorry. I didn't—"

"Do you realize the crisis she's caused in my home? She's made Mary hysterical. Do you realize that?"

Laspiti removed his cap and scratched at the sweat on his hairline. "I didn't know."

"I don't care what you knew. You make sure she doesn't come again." Agamemnon didn't look at his friend. "Now," he said, running his tongue across his teeth. "What was she talking about? What happened?"

Five men—all conservatives, loyal to the king—were killed the previous week. A representative of EAM/ELAS had invited the villagers to a meeting, held at the local campsite. They wanted to discuss collective plans for combatting the Germans, the man had said; he offered to cook meat.

The corpses were dumped in the village late that night. Four had been hanged, one shot at the base of the head.

"My God," Agamemnon said. He asked the names of the men, inquired about their widows. He realized that EAM/ELAS knew exactly which men to target: they'd killed Agamemnon's main allies. "They've been watching the villages," Agamemnon said.

"Unless they don't need to watch us: they might have someone who knows everyone already."

Agamemnon nodded and stared forward. A train was stalled on the tracks. Hundreds of fingers gripped the slats of the cattle cars; Agamemnon couldn't see the people's eyes, only their fingers.

"I was supposed to be there," Laspiti said. "But Constantia was... She miscarried again."

Agamemnon slumped. "Laspiti...I'm sorry," he said. "I'm sorry...about all of it."

The two men sat in the unmoving cart, unsure what to say. Agamemnon turned his head down, away from the train and Laspiti. "Has any counteraction been planned against EAM/ELAS?" he asked.

Laspiti sighed. "We can't go to the occupation authorities, and we can't go to the puppet government—they'd do nothing."

"No."

"But we can..." Laspiti paused.

"Go on."

"Well, there's talk in the village, as you can imagine."

"I can imagine."

"Because it was *barbaric* what they did. Barbaric! Bodies piled in the *platia*. A heap of men—of *men!*—for their families to see!"

Agamemnon smoothed his shirt, which Mary had clutched hours earlier. Hours? Minutes? The day had been too long already. "I'm not denying the brutality, Laspiti. I'm just asking what we can do."

"Well...you can imagine the talk, Agamemnon."

"I want you to say it."

"Well, they say..."

"I want *you* to say it."

Laspiti clamped his jaw. His teeth ground together as he spoke—bone on bone—his lips and tongue moving, exaggerated, trapped by his sealed jaw. "We can hunt them down in the mountains," he growled. "We can slaughter them."

Agamemnon nodded.

The metal wheels of the train squealed on the tracks. The cars started rolling toward Poland; the people inside said nothing.

"You could," Agamemnon said. "Very easily—you could. But I won't be a part of that. I don't believe in that form of justice."

Laspiti released his jaw. "And what do you believe in, Agamemnon? Please remind me, because I've suddenly lost my sense of direction."

Agamemnon nodded again. "Those bodies must have been disorienting, Laspiti. So let me remind you: I believe in the rule of law *if,*" he said, punctuating his point: "*if* the law is written with respect for order and human dignity."

"And where," Laspiti asked, "do we find such a law?"

Agamemnon looked to the train, which was gathering speed. The fingers soon began to blur, losing their distinction. "Perhaps only in our minds," he said. He turned to his friend, who was rubbing his face. His wedding band, thin and cheap, shone clean.

"And Constantia...has she recovered?" Agamemnon asked.

Laspiti lowered his hand to the reins. "Physically she's fine," he said. He paused. "She could see the fetus this time," he added. "It was a boy, Agamemnon.... He was a boy."

Papou Efstratios found Mary on the kitchen floor. She was lying on her side now, knees curled into her chest. Her nightgown was pulled askew; her left breast was mostly exposed, the mound of skin soft and unprotected. Papou Efstratios's eyes twitched as he looked at his daughter-in-law. The impulse to kick her was fierce.

"Get up, Mary," he said.

She recognized the tone of the command.

"I said get up." Papou Efstratios nudged the base of Mary's back with his foot. She rocked, her muscles not resisting. "Mary..."

Taki came inside now that his father was gone. He saw his grandfather's foot on the bottom of his mother's spine. "Stop it," he whispered.

"You woke me up with your screaming," Papou Efstratios said. "Your stupid screaming. You dare to scream at my son?"

Agamemnon's pencil had fallen onto the floor; the shavings were flaked around Mary's face.

"You dare to tell Agamemnon what to do? Huh?"

Taki watched his grandfather's foot prod Mary's back. "Stop, Papou.... Stop it."

Taki could feel his muscles fill with strength. He could feel his body charge forward, tackling the man, pinning his arms hard to the ground. He could feel his mouth call out: *Now, Mama— run! You're safe! Run now, Mama!*

"No..." he whimpered. "No... Mama...?"

Papou brought his foot back, fast, the leg bent at a right angle. "No!"

His mother's body jolted alive; her mouth sprang open in wordless pain.

"Get up," Papou said.

Mary rose to her hands and knees. Using the kitchen chair as a ladder, she slowly stood. Strands of hair were stuck to her cheek. Her lips were loose and wet. "Taki," she whispered, discovering him there, in the doorway. She clutched at her nightgown to cover her skin. She saw him say something, though she couldn't hear his voice. "What, Taki? What, my love?"

"Go outside," Papou Efstratios said. "Get me the newspaper."

Taki swallowed the dryness. "I…"

"Go!"

Taki ran, but not fast enough: before closing the door, he heard his mother grunt and fall.

Agamemnon did his work in the villages that day. He comforted the widows; he urged for calm, discipline and dignity, despite the calls for revenge. He returned home, as scheduled. Mary was preparing dinner, Taki was playing soccer, Papou Efstratios was reading the paper. No one referred to that morning. Eleni's visit and its aftermath were actively forgotten—an act that became less desperate as the weeks wore on—as Agamemnon worked in the villages, always returning home, his presence solid and true at the table beside his wife, whose black-and-blue marks had largely faded.

Twenty-Nine
Summer 1943

Agamemnon hadn't been sleeping well lately. Nothing was flowing properly: the British hadn't pursued Maki's initial contact, and the communists had stolen some pamphlets from the hideout where Yianni had stashed them. Costa, at least, had convinced some of his clients to support the exiled government. Agamemnon had, too. But that wasn't enough: one person at a time wasn't enough in this war.

Agamemnon's eyes were open against the darkness of the room. He was constructing his thoughts for the next meeting, to be held later that week. He could almost see his strategies building—his ideas like blocks of stone and wood that constructed a solid plan of action, which he then dismissed as untenable. He turned over and curled into Mary.

"My love," he whispered, his lips barely raised above her skin. He looked down the length of her sleeping body. His palm floated above her, close to her warmth. "My beauty..."

Agamemnon felt himself awakening into this, the one thing that would help him to sleep. He eased closer to his wife. "Mary, my love..." He heard a knocking at the door downstairs.

"Doctor Apostolides?" a voice called.

Agamemnon ignored the voice and its implications. He put his hand on Mary's hip, pushing down, into the muscle. She moaned—still asleep—an opening of breath through her throat. He felt her body reach back, into his.

"Doctor!"

"No..." Agamemnon groaned.

Mary rolled onto her back, her shoulders flat on the pillow. Her gold chain was slashed across her neck; the cross lay in the vulnerable dip of skin.

"Doctor Apostolides! Are you there? Are you awake?" The knocking became more insistent. "Please! I need your help!"

Agamemnon felt his hard-edged sleep recede. He picked up Mary's cross, holding it tight in his fist.

"Doctor! The labour has been too long! My cow, she's in trouble! Please!"

Mary nuzzled into the pillow.

"Doctor!"

Agamemnon placed the cross back on Mary's chest, pressing down. His hand straddled both sides of her neck, his thumb atop her sleeping pulse.

"Doctor!" The banging resumed.

"One minute," Agamemnon grumbled. He knew who was downstairs: this farmer's cow had gone through several menstrual cycles without becoming pregnant. Agamemnon had prescribed some tinctures for fertility, and located a bull from a different village. The farmer's wife had wept when she'd heard the cow was pregnant. The family needed the extra milk, or the bull to sell or barter.

"Doctor!" And now, two years after the process began, the time for the birth had come.

"One *minute*, I said."

Agamemnon trudged down the stairs, buckling his belt along the way. He wanted the banging to stop; he didn't want Mary to wake now that he was leaving for the villages. It was easier just to slip out.

"Doctor," the man proclaimed when Agamemnon opened the door. His fist was upraised, prepared to bang again. "It's my cow, it's—"

"I heard."

"It's been twenty-four hours, and the calf isn't—"

"Let me gather my tools. I'll be there in a minute."

"Please hurry. She's in distress, and—"

"I must—" Agamemnon said, his voice overly steady. "I must gather my tools. I'll meet you outside." He closed the door, reminding himself not to be annoyed.

Agamemnon packed his medical bag in the basement, bringing scalpels, rags, soap, sutures, the twist, and some ropes. He tore the bottom off a piece of paper on which Yianni had written an agenda for the meeting of the officers. Agamemnon wanted to leave a note for Mary. He dipped the nib of his pen into the inkwell.

Mary—
There is a cow in dystocia. I'll be home for dinner.
Love, Agamemnon

The note was hastily written. A blob of ink fell on the paper; hours would pass before a skin formed over its top.

"Doctor!"

Agamemnon strode upstairs, into the hallway. "What is he doing," he muttered. "I said I'd gather my—"

"Careful be!" Yiayia Loukia said. She put out her hand, preventing Agamemnon from charging into her.

"Mama! I'm sorry, I didn't know—"

"Where you are ing-go, Agamemnon?" Her breasts hung down, indistinguishable from the other tubes of fat on her torso.

"I have an appointment in the village, Mama."

"Okay. Bring me melon-water and cheese."

"I'll try, Mama." She smiled with a sweet emptiness that disturbed him. "Go back to bed, Mama. It's early."

"Yes, I know."

"I'll be back by dinner."

"Stay don't too late," she said. She stepped aside to let her son pass. "We'll wait for you."

The cow was tied to a chestnut tree on a field behind the farmer's house. The rope was connected from the animal's neck to the ring driven into the tree's bark. She took trembling steps, gingerly pacing on the grass; stillness was more painful than motion.

Agamemnon climbed off the cart and approached the cow. She was visible in the lantern light, a lone figure alive, bright against the black background. "Could you see that before you left?" Agamemnon asked, pointing to the hooves that poked out of the cow's vagina.

"No. That's new."

"Good," Agamemnon said. "Give me a minute to prepare, and we'll begin."

The farmer took the lantern and turned the light toward the barn, with its stone fountain and low slate-top table. "Pardon the mess," he apologized. The barn doors were flung open, the horse's stall untidy. The farmer had obviously left in a rush. Across from the stall, several goats slept on the compact dirt floor. The manure pile beside them was low, the contents largely spread on the fields.

Agamemnon lit a second lantern, which was hung from a hook attached to a wooden beam. The lantern swung as he released his hands. Shadows were projected over the barn; they swayed on the walls, the floors, the bodies of the animals and men. Agamemnon washed his hands and arms, up to the shoulder. The soap foamed white on his skin; the water was the vibrant cold of underground. "Put the stool by the cow," Agamemnon directed. "This may take a while." The farmer nodded.

A scrawny cat sussed out Agamemnon with glowing eyes. She stood from her nest and crawled obliquely toward him, shoulder blades raised on her grey body. Her belly drooped low;

she was heavy with milk and protruding nipples. Her kittens' eyes were still closed. Only one had died so far.

Agamemnon sat on the stool behind the cow. He grabbed her tail and pulled it to the side. "Hold her head—keep her still," he told the farmer. He then slid his hand into the vaginal duct, reaching past the calf's legs, the cow's cervix, into the uterus. His fingers spread along the sodden tissue of the uterine wall. He pressed his nails through the gunk onto the muscle; his fingers scraped down.

"Keep her steady," he commanded. He continued to scrape, attempting to induce a contraction. "Steady." He could feel the muscle start to respond—a slow hardening, the fibres fisting. Agamemnon pushed his arm further, his biceps swallowed into the cow. The base of the uterus encircled his arm, constricting; his fingertips went numb.

"Well, we know the uterus isn't fatigued," he said.

He removed his arm before the contraction gripped too tight. Clotted blood was dragged out with him. It fell onto the grass and split.

"So what's the problem, doctor?"

"I'm not sure," he said, shaking out his arm. Bits of mucus sprayed through the air. "I'll have to check around some more." Agamemnon waited for the contraction to pass before going back in. While he paused he looked east, toward the foothills. The morning's rays warmed the sky with diffuse orange light. The sun, in its ball of strength, hadn't yet risen over the mountains. Agamemnon thought of Mary in their bed. He hoped she was still sleeping; he felt a surge of wanting to be there, asleep beside her.

The cow stepped, wobbly, as the contraction passed. Agamemnon took a preparatory breath and pushed back in. This time he groped around the calf's head. He felt the cranium beneath the mucus membranes. He let his palm flow slick over the hollows and rises of the calf's face; his fingers then searched further, onto the soft muscle of the calf's neck.

"Well, there's the problem," he said. "The head is positioned improperly."

"What does that mean?"

"That means I have to adjust the position of the head." He peered over the large protrusion of pelvic bone. "And you have to hold her steady, understand?"

"I understand."

"Get the twist."

Agamemnon removed his arm again. The uterus had to be relaxed for him to execute this next procedure: namely, pushing the calf's hooves back in, then changing the way the animal was angled in the cow's body. He knew this action would distress the cow; she'd start to swing her pelvis around, with his arm inside her, unless the farmer could successfully use the twist.

The man didn't have much experience with the tool, but its mechanics seemed clear. He took it from the table in the barn. The noose was small, tied to the end of a rod that fit, thick, in his palm.

"So: the twist," Agamemnon instructed. "Put the noose around the lip, then wait for me to give you the word."

"Then...?"

"Then twist the rod as fast as you can. The rope will keep the lip pinched. It'll distract her from what's going on back here. Because if we can distract her—"

Agamemnon heard a woman's laughter. The farmer's wife had entered the barn, carrying a tall glass of water for each of the men. "Distract her," she said, and laughed again. The sound was light in the blood and dirt of that morning. "I don't think anything can distract the poor beast now!"

Agamemnon smiled at the woman. Her hair was black and curled around her face. "No," Agamemnon said. "I guess not."

The woman gave her husband a quick kiss and returned indoors. She would go to the fields with her daughter now; the sun would soon rise on their strong, bent backs.

Agamemnon watched the cow cycle through another contraction. He watched the pelvis tighten, slow, solidify—squeezed from the inside—then rush into release.

"Now," he commanded. "Do it now." He reached deep into the womb and spread his hand over the calf's neck. He leaned his chest forward, his arm locked and taut. He pushed against the nature of birth. The cow lowed and whipped Agamemnon with her tail; its bone hit Agamemnon's back; the hairs—clumped with blood and birth and mud—slashed Agamemnon's cheek. "Damn it, tighten the twist!"

The farmer placed the twist before the cow's mouth. With one hand, he extended the animal's lip through the noose; with the other, he twirled the rod. The rope constricted around the delicate tissue. The cow jerked her head in a tight spasm and fell still.

Agamemnon had risen off the stool; the muscles of his gut and legs engaged, holding him steady. His feet pressed down, into the ground, as his hand pressed forward. He strained with the force of the dirt and the womb; he pushed in opposite directions, his body linking the two.

"Tighten!" he grunted. "Tighter!"

The calf was taken into the uterus. Without pause, Agamemnon shifted the position of the head. The neck did not resist; this body—supple and warm—was not yet tensed with its own life.

Mary awoke in an empty bed. She stretched her arms wide, luxuriant. She let out one pulse of a moan. "What time is it?" she wondered aloud. She swung her legs out of bed, pausing before she stood and removed her nightgown, letting it flutter down. Agamemnon was right: she *had* lost weight since the war began.

She hadn't been able to wear that nightgown since she'd become pregnant with Taki, eleven years ago. The white silk fabric was bolted over the breasts and cut close along the hips. It cooled her—quenched her, almost—whenever it touched her skin.

The morning was sultry for mid-July. Mary walked naked to her armoire and selected a light blue skirt. Musing that this might fit her again, too, she stepped into the garment and shimmied it over the curve of her hips. She fastened the buttons and ran her hand over her belly. "Very nice." She smiled, looking at herself in the mirror. She swivelled to see herself in profile, the blue skirt fitted over her legs, her chest bare. "He'll like this."

"He's gone."

Mary spun around and crossed her arms over her breasts. "What?" Her mother-in-law stood in the doorway. "What did you say?"

"Gone he is." Yiayia Loukia smiled and tilted her head. "You're very pretty," she said. "And who are you?"

Agamemnon observed the cow through several contractions: he wanted the labour to find its own flow now that the calf was positioned properly. Besides, the men needed to rest before the final phase of birth.

Agamemnon sat with his back against the wall of the barn. His knees were bent, his eyes closed. The farmer tried to insist that Agamemnon take his bed, but Agamemnon refused: he didn't want to fall into true sleep—not until he was home, in his own bed, beside Mary. "I need to be near the animal," he said. "I'll just rest my eyes a minute. Just a minute...."

It was early afternoon when the mother cat woke him. Her tongue was scraping over his forearm, tasting the salt and blood. "Scat!" he said, shooing her away. He rubbed his forearm and sighed. He shouldn't have drifted for so long.

"The contractions are coming every minute or so," the farmer said, approaching Agamemnon with a glass of water.

Agamemnon drank the water down, saving the last cold drops to rub on his face. "Okay. Well. Let's see what we've got," he said.

Taki played soccer alone in the yard, dribbling past pretend defenders. He kicked his homemade rag ball with the inside of his big toe, just as Dimitra had taught him. The ball lifted: the rags flew apart, like a bird being shot, its feathers floating to the ground. Taki gathered the bits of the ball. Without complaint, he sat in the grass and patiently tried to retie them.

Loukia stood on the backyard verandah. She watched her brother; his silence agitated her. "Did you hear anything this morning?"

"No." Taki chose two short rags to join together.

"You didn't hear *anything*?"

Taki looked up at his sister, the frayed rags in his hands. He knew, then, to be afraid—more afraid than normal—specifically afraid, at this moment, now. "No," he said, small.

"Someone banged at the door. He was yelling for Daddy."

"I didn't hear it."

"It was loud."

"I didn't hear it. Maybe you were—"

"I *heard* it, Taki."

Loukia descended the stairs and sat cross-legged on the grass. Together the siblings reconstructed the soccer ball. Every few minutes, Loukia would walk inside to search the house for their father.

"He's not back yet," she'd report to Taki each time. "Not yet." Then they would return to their silent work.

The sun was at its hottest when the labour quickened into transition. Agamemnon retrieved a rope from the barn.

"Should I use the twist?" the farmer asked.

"No," Agamemnon replied. "We don't need it anymore. We can't change what'll come now."

Agamemnon grabbed the calf's two front legs, which again protruded from the vagina. He tied the hooves together, then wrapped the rope several times around his hand. He waited for the next contraction. When the hardening came, he leaned back, into the air; the rope kept him suspended. This was the end, he knew.

Mary was preparing another vegetable soup. She'd decided to use her last stick of cinnamon bark—a special treat for Agamemnon. She'd been saving the bark for months, ever since Taki had returned from Levon's store with a container of spices and herbs— largely unusable, of course, all mixed up as they were. But the cinnamon was salvageable. And she would use it now—now that Agamemnon had gone to the villages for a pre-dawn emergency. "He's gone," his mother had said. She'd chirped it, actually, her voice pure in its simplicity, its detachment from all the twisted tendrils that might link it to other thoughts, or fears, or implications. Yes, Agamemnon was gone. But he'd be back by dinner, of course. The note on the countertop said so. *...cow in dystocia. I'll be home for dinner. Love, Agamemnon*

Mary plunged the potatoes into a bucket of water and scrubbed them with a stiff brush. Her palms were soon covered with a layer of grit, her forearms splattered in brown.

Papou Efstratios came into the kitchen, his hands in the pockets of his trousers. "I want my coffee now."

Mary sighed and set the scrub brush on the counter. "Right away." The noise of her thoughts quieted as she tended to her father-in-law's demands. She boiled water in the *briki*, then dumped a heap of chickpea powder inside. A pool of water formed beneath the head of the scrub brush. The puddle's beaded edge expanded toward the note. Papou Efstratios peered into the sink.

"Potatoes again?"

Mary watched the chickpea coffee begin to foam in thick blond bubbles. "Yes, Papou. With cinnamon this time," she said, pouring the coffee.

"Cinnamon..." Papou Efstratios grimaced and walked back to the parlour to finish the newspaper while sipping his scalding beverage.

Mary closed her eyes, exhausted by this day, which had started so strangely—caught naked by her mother-in-law—and had proceeded in the same jarring rhythm. She felt she could fall asleep standing up, drift off into dreams. Her body swayed.

The note on the counter absorbed the pool of water in one greedy pull. Agamemnon's penmarks became bloated. *I'll be home Love*

The mother licked the membranes off her child, then nudged the calf to standing. By the time Agamemnon had washed the blood from his skin, the calf was latched to the mother's teat. "Another female," Agamemnon said, drying his forearms. "We'll be back in two years for *her* labour."

"God willing," the farmer said, making the sign of the cross.

Agamemnon wanted to return home—to dinner and his own table, to Mary and his bed. He needed to complete some work in the village, though: EAM/ELAS's membership was increasing fast, according to Maki's information; now was the perfect moment to combat that trend here, in this village, whose fortunes Agamemnon had visibly changed. The calf was clear evidence that the king's government cared about the people; its wobbly presence would be more convincing than any argument about sovereignty or tradition or radical Russian manifestos.

"Would you like some food, doctor? Please stay. I don't believe you've ever sat at my table."

"I haven't? Well, that must change." Agamemnon smiled to cover his weariness.

The farmer's family had recently returned from the fields. The girl prepared the table on the verandah, while the wife whisked up a meal: farm eggs and bread, which she'd baked that morning, kneading the dough as her husband had banged on Agamemnon's door.

Agamemnon took a large bite of yellow egg.

"In two years," the farmer mused. "Where will we be in two years."

The evening sun penetrated the grapevines; it was bright in Agamemnon's eyes. "You have good land, a good wife and *two* cows. You should be fine."

"But the *country*. Where will the *country* be, doctor? Do you think this war will be over in three years?"

"That depends," Agamemnon said. "Which war do you mean?"

Other villagers were visiting the house on their way back from the fields. They congratulated the farmer on his new calf; he credited Agamemnon.

"Which war do *you* mean, doctor?" one of the farmers asked. Almost a dozen had gathered by now. They'd been silent all day, alone with their crops and thoughts and fatiguing muscle. Now they wanted the sharp play of conversation.

"Not the war against the Nazis—that war's fate is already written," Agamemnon said. "No: I mean the war where we eat our own children."

One of the farmers pulled his strand of worry beads from his pocket.

"We should be nurturing our country, with our own tradition and history and values." Agamemnon gestured toward the back of the house, where the cow was nursing her calf. "Others disagree, of course: others want to suckle off Mother Russia, but that teat is dry. Russia will turn on us. She'll suck from our veins."

"But...I don't know, doctor," one farmer said, leaning forward in his chair. "I hear that ELAS is separate from Russia. I hear they're for the people—the *Greek* people."

The farmer replaced Agamemnon's water with ouzo.

Agamemnon twirled his glass. "Tell me exactly what you hear," he said. "Because I hear otherwise." He took the liquid down his throat.

Mary lowered the flame under the pot. She'd decided to delay the meal, in case Agamemnon was close to home, which he should be.... *home for dinner.* Yiayia Loukia sighed like a song from her perch on the parlour couch. Papou Efstratios guffawed at something he read in the paper.

Mary adjusted the cutlery on the table, flipping all the knives so their blades faced in, toward the space where the food would go. She considered eating her allocated slice of bread, but resolved to wait until Agamemnon arrived, so they could all eat together.

Taki and Loukia came inside the parlour. "He's not here yet?" Loukia asked her grandfather; he grunted a reply.

Mary noticed the veins on the back of her hand, five of them thrusting up in bumps and gnarls, turgid across the bones. She straightened Agamemnon's fork, which was crooked. When she was satisfied with its position, she lifted her finger; the metal stuck to her skin, jostling the fork out of place. She tried again.

"Did you hear the door this morning, Papou?" Loukia asked. "Because I'm sure I heard it.... Papou? Papou, did you hear it?"

The third time Mary tried to straighten the fork, she used two hands: one at the foot, one at the prongs. She swivelled it back and forth, with increasing precision, then lifted her fingers. It skimmed to the left.

"*I* heard it," Yiayia Loukia said.

Mary picked up the fork and slammed it onto the table. "Stay!" she screamed.

"*I* heard it: Boom-boom-boom-boom." Yiayia Loukia rocked back and forth on the couch. "Boom-boom-boom-boom. 'Doctor!'" she called, her hand to her jowl. "'Doctor, where are you?' Boom-boom-boom-boom."

"Stay!" Mary screamed. "Agamemnon!"

"Boom-boom-boom-boom."

"When will dinner be ready?" Papou Efstratios demanded.

Taki found his sister's hand.

"Agamemnon!"

The workhorse plodded toward Thessaloniki. Agamemnon felt himself carried by the crackling sound of wheels that rolled over the pebbled road. The horse was slow: Agamemnon would be late. He hoped Mary wouldn't be worried.

"Look at that," the farmer said, pointing to Mount Olympus. The peak seemed to pierce the sun's underbelly; the evening light shot in striations across the mountainside.

"Yes, it's very nice," Agamemnon replied. He was too tired to attend to the beauty of a mountain.

"Doctor!" a man called. "Doctor Apostolides!"

"Again..." he sighed.

Fifteen hours ago, the farmer beside him had banged on his door; now the pounding was from horses' hooves along the road, the sound getting louder as the animals overtook the farmer's cart. There were two of them. They cut off the farmer's horse.

"Doctor! Doctor Apostolides, we've been looking for you!" This man was tanned, and young. Agamemnon did not know him.

"What's the problem?"

His horse was sick, he said—frothing at the mouth, he said—in a barn, not far away. He needed the doctor's help, urgently.

"Where's the horse?" Agamemnon directed the question toward the second man, whose gaze gave off an intensity of aggression that seemed familiar.

"It's in a barn. Just like he said."

"Okay," Agamemnon said, sleep receding. "But where's the barn?"

"That question is irrelevant," the man said. He drove his heels into the horse's flanks while yanking hard on the reins. The horse gave a gallop, in place.

"Doctor..." the farmer warned.

"You're the Alexiou boy, aren't you," Agamemnon said, placing the man's face now. "Tell me: how is your father?"

Aleko Alexiou snuffled reflexively; he swallowed the phlegm and spit a wad onto the ground. "My father's fine. I don't see him much."

"That's too bad. He's a good man."

Aleko smiled through the bristles of his brown facial hair. The muscles around his eyes remained unmoving.

"Please!" the first man interrupted. "This horse is all my family has. My wife is pregnant. What will we do without this horse?"

"I don't recognize you," Agamemnon said, turning toward that man. "What village are you from?"

"Doctor..." the farmer said again. This situation obviously wasn't right. The farmer couldn't straighten it in his mind; he couldn't arrange the story and players, the motives and strategies. He knew Agamemnon was in danger, though. And the longer he stayed there—there, with these men, in the middle of the empty farm fields—the more he was in danger, too. The taste of eggs rose through his chest and filled his mouth. "Doctor..."

"I just moved here, from Athens," the man said. "Conditions are bad there."

Agamemnon nodded. "From Athens," he repeated. "Funny, you sound like you're from Macedonia."

"Athens," Aleko stated. "He's my cousin from Athens. I'm helping him get accustomed to local issues."

Agamemnon squinted. "And how's that going—getting accustomed?"

"He's taking on new challenges all the time."

"Doctor, please, I must take you home," the farmer pleaded. "You've done your duty, now I must do mine. I *must* take you home."

"*We'll* take him home. Don't worry," Aleko said. "Besides, you should be getting back to that beautiful daughter of yours. She's really grown up, hasn't she? Such luscious curls on that girl."

The farmer shut his eyes. Flashing in his vision was Aleko's orange afterimage. That strobe was soon soothed by a shadow: Agamemnon was stepping off the cart, his medical bag in hand.

"You go home," he said to the farmer. "This isn't about you right now. Go home before that changes."

The farmer hesitated. He watched Agamemnon tie his bag to the saddle of Aleko's horse.

"Do you mind if I ride her?" Agamemnon asked Aleko. "You can ride with your...your cousin...."

Aleko stood in the stirrups. He paused, staring down at Agamemnon, his hips pushed forward. Without answering, he swung one leg over the animal and arced to the ground. "Go ahead," Aleko said. He came to full height, his chest close to Agamemnon's. "Enjoy the ride, Officer Apostolides."

The farmer gripped the reins as he sat in his cart. "Doctor..." he said. "Doctor, this isn't..."

"Go home," Agamemnon insisted. He mounted the horse. "Go home to your family."

Mary sat on the couch in the parlour that night. She sat on the couch and brushed her hair. Some time long after dark, she washed her hair in the bathroom sink. She washed her hair and put on a fresh dress. In her fresh dress, she brushed her clean hair. She wouldn't panic until morning.

All the while, Taki slept. Loukia tossed but Taki slept, and he would wonder about this, decades later: he would wonder, aloud, about his capacity to sleep on such a night.

Epilogue

History, Memory, Story

He was killed moments later. He was hanged in an abandoned barn, his corpse dumped in a nearby ravine. We know this fact because of the killer's hubris: Aleko Alexiou came riding into Laspiti's village that night. Legs astride his horse, he looked down at Constantia as she stood in her garden.

"Who will baptize your child now?" he asked.

"Agamemnon Apostolides."

"Agamemnon Apostolides is dead."

It was then that she noticed the clothes Aleko wore.

"He will baptize my child!" she insisted, frantic.

Aleko laughed and smoothed his shirt: Agamemnon's shirt, stripped from the still-warm corpse. Aleko's hand rubbed his thigh as Constantia looked away.

My grandfather's body was never found.

(Aleko Alexiou was not his name.)

For fourteen months, the family thought Agamemnon might be alive. Laspiti urged them to abandon hope. "We know he's dead," he'd say, gentle and caring, and Mary would spit in his face.

"Bring me *proof!*" she'd rage. "Bring me a *body* to mourn, and then I'll believe!"

Laspiti never told her about the clothes and Aleko's night-time declaration of murder. He thought that image was too rank. He wanted to spare her the awful intimacy of the murder scene and its aftermath. But my father wishes Laspiti had conveyed that information. He thinks that would've been proof enough. Instead, the family continued to believe that Agamemnon might be alive. They believed the words of communists who came occasionally to their door, expressing their regret that Agamemnon couldn't yet return home, explaining that he was their hostage, highly valued for his veterinary skills. They assured Mary that Agamemnon would be released at the end of the war, once the Germans were defeated. They told her he was safe, and well. "He sends his love," the communist would say, taking Mary's hand. "He asks only for a few tools to aid in his work. His scalpels, perhaps, and also his winter boots...."

The family believed.

For a day, or a week, or a month, they celebrated Agamemnon's life, overjoyed by the promise of his eventual return. They celebrated fully until Laspiti, again, arrived. "He's dead," he would say, and Mary would scream, and the family, again, would mourn. For a day. Or a week. Or a month. Until a communist arrived.

This occurred for over a year.

Alive-dead. Alive-dead. Alive-dead.

My father waited.

Alive-dead. Alive-dead.

The family accepted Agamemnon's death only on the day when the Germans fled, leaving Thessaloniki in a solemn procession. The young soldiers marched directly into an ambush on the city's outskirts. Hundreds were killed, including Private Benedikt.

(Benedikt was not his name. He loved to play the piano.)

That German procession was followed by a mass celebration on the streets of the city. People poured from their homes, rejoicing in the end of war and occupation. The communists flooded the city, too, down from their hidden camps in the mountains. They paraded along the main boulevards in a spontaneous act of triumph later labelled the Freedom Day Parade.

This would be the day.

On this day, they would see their father.

"Did you really believe he was alive?"

"Of course we believed!" my father replied. "It was plausible—it was possible they were holding him hostage.... It made sense! And we wanted to believe...."

In preparation for Agamemnon's arrival, Loukia wore a special dress. She asked Katarina to braid her hair. "I wanted to look beautiful for my father," she said.

(Katarina and Maki were not their names.)

The family waited all day.

They stood outside, among the celebrants. My father climbed the iron gate at the entrance to the house. From here, he could look down upon the men—hundreds of men, their faces dirty with sweat and earth, their hair unkempt and wild. Communist men, from the mountains. Men who took his father.

My father searched these faces, anticipating the moment of recognition. He waited, his body lithe and alert, anticipating. This was my father's experience.

I cannot hold that experience in my body. I cannot make myself stay, as he stayed, his body patient but longing atop the gate, waiting. He was still a child.

This was the day they knew Agamemnon was dead.

(Panayiotis Panayiotidis was his name.)

Panayiotis was killed by machine-gun fire.

Panayiotis had established a right-wing youth organization in 1946, when the Civil War was intensifying. He invited my father to join, but my father deferred and demurred, promising Panayiotis he'd stop by soon. He never did, of course. My father didn't want to get involved; he didn't have the desire for vengeance or violence. But always he promised: soon.

The following year, several communist youth attacked the group's headquarters. They pounded on the door, yelling for the boys to come down and fight. Panayiotis thrust the door open, his knife cocked and ready; the communists immediately started firing. Five teens were killed, falling atop each other—a heap of young men piled at the threshold. My father was afraid to attend the funeral; he was afraid he'd be spotted and targeted by the communists in the next round of attacks. This fact causes my father great shame.

Panayiotis had grey eyes.

(Loukia Apostolides was her name.)

Loukia emigrated to Toronto as a young wife. She is now known by a different name—Lucy Grigoriadis—but she is the same person. The girl who volunteered in hospitals and organized plays became the woman who worked tirelessly for the Greek immigrant community. As a social worker, mother and friend, Lucy has created a culture of pride among Greeks in the Diaspora. She has established an international reputation for her good work; closer to home, she has taught me the meaning of generosity and forgiveness.

(Mary Apostolides was her name.)

Mary Apostolides—my Yiayia Mary—guided me into this project. I began by interviewing her because I wasn't yet ready to talk to my father, to feel his stories and emotions. We were still too close; I still needed him to be a stable figurehead, not a man with a history determined by chance and will. But Yiayia I could ask. She was a wonderful mystery to me, a woman of another place, whose spirit nonetheless felt like home.

Toward the end of her life, Yiayia Mary told me many tiny secrets; some of these I've kept to myself.

(Philip Samsarelos was his name.)

Philip married a village girl named Sophia, despite his mental instability. He fathered two children before dying in 1952, deliberately succumbing to a mild case of tuberculosis. By all accounts, he could've recovered if he'd cared for himself. But Philip wanted to die: he'd wanted to die for years. He needed the honesty of death.

Of all the characters who populate this book, Philip is the one with whom I've fallen deeply, madly in love.

(The newsagent's son does not have a name in this story.)

None of us ever knew the name of this man—the man with the vile glare and large Adam's apple. This man knew my father, though: "We got your father, Taki Apostolides," he used to say. He'd point to my father as he walked past the store, toward the dairy. "We got your father," he continued, "and we can get you, too." This my father remembers: those words, that throat, the finger pointed at his chest. This man joined the communist army in 1946. My father assumes he died during the war.

This war, the Greek Civil War, lasted until 1949. At its end, one-third of the Greek population was either dead or displaced.

"One-third of the Greek population was either dead or displaced."

I need to imagine the meaning of this number.

One-third—one in three—dead or homeless.

Agamemnon—Mary—Taki.

Panayiotis—Nikos—Loukia.

Philip—Levon—Laspiti.

One in three: the whole country had cause to grieve.

My father never grieved—not actively, as least. "My feelings were kind of dead for a long time," he told me.

(Constantia Laspiti was her name.)

The Laspitis' first child, following multiple miscarriages, was baptized by my father. The ceremony became a political event, with royalists gathering at the church, heralding this child as a good omen. The crowd was too vast to be contained in the church; instead, the girl was baptized on the *platia*, on the spot where the corpses had been dumped three years earlier. My father said he felt like a shadow.

"It was *him* who should've been there," he said. "My father should have been there, and they all knew it."

My father felt like a shadow.

He was a boy in the shadow of his dead father.

His father was dead, and yet *he* was the ghost.

"We all knew it: the honour wasn't *mine*. It wasn't *me*. I did nothing to deserve that honour. Quite the contrary...."

My father had failed to avenge his father's death. If he'd wanted to seek revenge, he wouldn't have been punished. But vengeance wasn't his way—his fate and pulse. Instead of acting through violence, my father forced himself to stand in the place of honour, baptizing a new life.

(Dimitri Laspiti was his name.)

Dimitri continued in his leadership role. When the communists surrendered in 1949, Dimitri assumed a political position in the countryside. He worked to prevent acts of revenge, which had become rampant, particularly among the royalists. For years, these men burned communists' homes, raped women, tortured men. Beheadings were not uncommon. Dimitri declared that this would end: he would not allow this form of justice. He died in the 1990s, an old man revered in the villages. He'd reportedly wanted to shake my father's hand before he died.

(Nikos Hadzis was his name.)

Nikos didn't shake my dad's hand, either. Instead, he embraced him fully.

My father hadn't spoken with Nikos since the day he boarded a ship in 1949, travelling to America alone. Fifty-three years later, he picked up a telephone in Thessaloniki, a thick phonebook spread on his lap. We'd arrived in Greece six hours earlier; this was my father's first trip home. He'd come because of me.

"Is this Nikos?" he asked. "Nikos Hadzis, from Gondicas's school?"

I listened from the hallway; I heard my father's laughter.

"Don't go anywhere," Nikos replied. "I'm coming right now."

They told stories that night, for hours, and again the next day. I couldn't understand their words—I have never learned to speak Greek—but I understood the tone, the gestures; I understood their glorious laughter. I have never heard my father laugh so freely as he did that night with Nikos Hadzis, his best friend from childhood.

That night, I wept for his lost freedom.

This was not his story anymore.

This was not my book. It was his life.

This life, I realized, was cut in two, its continuity severed in 1949. When my father immigrated to America, he sealed off all thoughts of his past.

"That life was over," he said and slapped his palm on the table. "It was over. Period. Until..."

"Until?"

"Until *you* started asking questions. Until then, I avoided it. I suppressed it, I avoided it, I ran away from it. I didn't deal with what my life was and had been. I just did what I had to do, every day, putting one foot in front of the other."

One foot in front of the other, my father learned the language, earned money to help his uncle Apostolus, attended a local college. Apostolus wanted him to work in the fur factory, but my father requested one chance before he agreed to that life: he would send one single application to veterinary school. Cornell University Veterinary School, the best in the country. If he got rejected, he'd become the factory's floor manager. That was the deal: one chance.

He was accepted.

Within ten years of graduation, he'd married a first-generation Greek-American, opened the largest veterinary hospital on Long Island and fathered two children. His past in Greece was over. Period.

(Dimitra was not her name.)

My father was loved by this bold girl. She gave him her young, romantic love: a crush, a flirtation, an innocent delirium. This was the only love she'd ever know.

Dimitra died of meningitis, falling ill on Monday and dying on Thursday.

She was a tomboy with brown hair and a crooked smile, whose body was ease and strength—instinctual knowledge— who played like a pro in my father's backyard.

My father can't remember this girl's name. He remembers, instead, how she ran and smiled. He remembers how she died. He went to see her that day. She was lying in bed, surrounded by adults who hovered above, useless. He shouldn't have gone: she was highly contagious, certain to die, certainly delirious. She wouldn't even know he'd been there, Nikos said; he could get deathly sick for nothing. He shouldn't go.

He went.

"Why did you go? If you knew she was contagious..."

"You go to see whether it was true—to find out what was happening. And to communicate, too.... You realize what communication meant—how important it was to say what you felt or thought.'"

He walked up the stairs to her room. The stairwell was narrow, dark; he stood near the top, leaning against the wall. She lay in her deathbed: she, the girl who loved him.

"But there were no words. We didn't exchange any words...." They exchanged, instead, gazes. "There was recognition in her eyes," he said. He was quiet, looking down, unable to take my gaze. "These were not the 'absent eyes' of meningitis."

"She saw me."

I love him.

I see him now as a man—my father—a boy, a man, who kept his stories silent, who acted bravely when it mattered. He saw, in a relationship with a brown-haired girl who needed him, loved him: he saw, and let himself be seen.

(Marianne Apostolides is my name.)

On our return trip to Greece—the culmination of seven years of research, forty-seven interview tapes, sheaves of words written and read—my father visited the sites of his childhood. We went to the village where Agamemnon was killed. We sat with Constantia Laspiti on the verandah of her daughter's home, surrounded by wheat fields and olive trees, foothills and ravines. His father's body had long since decayed, absorbed into the countryside, becoming the land. That day, we raised our glasses in a toast to Agamemnon.

(Agamemnon Apostolides was his name.)

We visited Zagora, too, where we watched children play hide-and-seek in the *platia*, their small bodies scurrying inside the hollow plane trees. One of those children was my daughter, aged two; I was pregnant, at the time, with my son.

They will know this story; my children's challenge—the story they'll seek and tell—will be different.

(Yiayia Evantheia and Papou Yiorgos Samsarelos were their names.)

Finally, we visited my father's old neighbourhood in Thessaloniki. He found the apartment building where Spiros once lived; the remnants of the low stone wall where Levon had spread his coffee beans; the cypress trees in front of Gondicas's school. All the gorgeous homes with their frescoes and grand staircases, their archways and iron gates—all had been torn down. Nothing, my father said, was the same.

He seemed bewildered as we wandered; he was far more lost than I.

(Spiros, Levon, Gondicas: these were not their names.)

He came to Greece because of me. He re-entered his past because I insisted on knowing. For years, I grappled with the material of my father's life: memories and history, details alongside broad generalizations:

The bomb shelter smelled like wet concrete.

The garbage carts squealed when their load was heavy.

The horse's agonized bellow rumbled in his chest.

I failed to honour my father's name.

(Efstratios Agamemnon "Taki" Apostolides is his name.)

For years I tried to capture my father's past in a single, true narrative. I tried to lock our lives into a stable structure we could both understand. I tried, and failed, because I hadn't yet learned to trust: not myself, not our love, not language. I wanted, too much, to give him his past: to redeem this tragedy in some resplendent truth.

I wanted, and failed, and tried again, for twelve years.

And through this need to understand the past, I finally came to create a story. I finally *became* my own fate and luck— my own essential desire to question and create, to form meaning through language.

Our stories, now, are intertwined. They exceed history and memory. They exceed ourselves. This is their truth.

Marianne Apostolides is a writer and critic. Her first book, *Inner Hunger: A Young Woman's Struggle through Anorexia and Bulimia*, was published by W. W. Norton and translated into Spanish and Swedish. Her novel *Swim* (BookThug, 2009) explores the eroticism of language and story. She lives in Toronto with her two children.

BOOKS FROM MANSFIELD PRESS

Poetry
Leanne Averbach, *Fever*
Diana Fitzgerald Bryden, *Learning Russian*
Alice Burdick, *Flutter*
Margaret Christakos, *wipe.under.a.love*
Pino Coluccio, *First Comes Love*
Gary Michael Dault, *The Milk of Birds*
Pier Giorgio Di Cicco, *The Visible World*
Christopher Doda, *Aesthetics Lesson*
Rishma Dunlop, *Metropolis*
Suzanne Hancock, *Another Name for Bridge*
Jason Heroux, *Emergency Hallelujah*
Carole Glasser Langille, *Late in a Slow Time*
Jeanette Lynes, *The Aging Cheerleader's Alphabet*
David W. McFadden, *Be Calm, Honey*
Lillian Necakov, *The Bone Broker*
Peter Norman, *At the Gates of the Theme Park*
Catherine Owen & Joe Rosenblatt, with Karen Moe, *Dog*
Corrado Paina, *Souls in Plain Clothes*
Jim Smith, *Back Off, Assassin! New & Selected Poems*
Robert Earl Stewart, *Something Burned Along the Southern Border*
Steve Venright, *Floors of Enduring Beauty*
Brian Wickers, *Stations of the Lost*

Fiction
Marianne Apostolides, *The Lucky Child*
Kent Nussey, *A Love Supreme*
Tom Walmsley, *Dog Eat Rat*

Non-fiction
Pier Giorgio Di Cicco, *Municipal Mind*
Amy Lavender Harris, *Imagining Toronto*